WHISPERS OF THE HIGHLAND MOORS

DEE WHITMAN

WHISPERS OF THE HIGHLAND MOORS

Copyright © 2024 by Dee Whitman
Cover Design by DEW Media
Cover Artwork by DEW Media

ISBN 978-1-991296-00-9 Paperback
ISBN 978-1-991296-01-6 E-book

All rights reserved. No part of this book may be reproduced in any manner whatsoever without written permission except in the case of brief quotations embodied in critical articles and reviews.
DEW Media is a subsidiary of SKW Publishing.

First Printing, 2024
Second Printing, 2026

CONTENTS

PROLOGUE

The Highland winds carried stories.

They swept across the heather-clad hills, skimmed the surface of lochs, and wound through the valleys like voices searching for ears willing to listen. Most dismissed them as nothing more than the sounds of nature.

Elspeth knew better.

She stood upon the rise, her shawl pulled tight against the evening chill. Behind her, the standing stones loomed from the gathering mist, their weathered markings softened by time. The air felt different tonight. Heavy. Waiting.

The moors were restless.

A gust tore across the hillside, stirring the heather around her boots. Elspeth narrowed her eyes toward the western horizon.

Something was coming.

Not a storm. Not rain.

Something older.

Below, Maree Doonagan paused on the path leading home. The fading light cast long shadows across the land, turning familiar hills into dark silhouettes.

She stopped without knowing why.

A strange unease settled over her.

The Highlands had always felt alive to Maree. The land was as much a part of her as the blood in her veins. Yet tonight, it felt as though the hills themselves were watching.

Waiting.

Elspeth watched her in silence.

Many had crossed these moors over the years, leaving little more than footprints behind.

Maree was different.

She belonged here.

"Ye hear it, then?" Elspeth called quietly.

Maree glanced up.

"Hear what?"

"The land."

Maree hesitated.

"I dinnae hear anythin'."

"Nay." Elspeth smiled faintly. "But ye feel it."

The younger woman looked back toward the darkening hills.

"Aye," she admitted at last. "I do."

For a moment neither spoke.

The wind whispered through the heather.

"The moors have been waitin'," Elspeth said.

Maree frowned.

"For what?"

Elspeth's gaze drifted beyond her, toward the distant ridges where the last light lingered.

"For those who belong to them."

The answer made little sense, yet Maree felt a shiver trace its way down her spine.

Far beyond the croft, a solitary figure moved along the ridge.

Dougal McBeth.

Elspeth watched him with the same knowing expression.

Another soul standing at a crossroads.

Neither of them understood it yet.

But the land did.

A gust swept across the moor, carrying a whisper just beyond hearing.

Maree turned sharply.

"Did ye hear that?"

Elspeth rested a hand upon her shoulder.

"Aye."

The old woman's eyes never left the horizon.

"It's beginnin'."

The wind rose once more, weaving its way through stone and heather.

And the Highlands never whispered without reason.

THE CONFRONTATION

Dougal McBeth had always been good at leaving.

The thought sat heavily upon him as he stood atop the ridge, gazing across the vast sweep of Highland moorland stretched before him. Heather rippled beneath the wind like a purple sea, while distant mountains stood watch beneath a sky painted with the fading colours of evening.

Behind him lay the only place that had ever tempted him to stay.

Ahead lay another road.

Another departure.

Another excuse.

His jaw tightened.

The Highlands had a memory.

He had learned that long ago.

The land remembered every footstep, every promise, every soul who had called it home. The old folk said the hills carried stories in their bones, that the standing stones listened when no one else did.

Dougal had always dismissed such things.

Yet standing there now, he could not shake the feeling that the land itself was watching him.

Waiting.

Judging.

The wind pressed against his back as though urging him onward.

Leave.

That was what he did best.

He had spent years wandering from place to place, never staying long enough to belong anywhere. It was easier that way. Safer.

No roots.

No obligations.

No broken hearts.

At least, that had been the plan.

His gaze drifted toward the distant valley where the Doonagan croft sat nestled among rolling hills and ancient stone walls.

Doonagan land.

Good land.

Old land.

Generations of hands had worked that soil.

Generations of stories lay buried beneath it.

And somehow, without intending to, he'd allowed himself to become part of it.

That had been his mistake.

A sound carried across the moor.

Hoofbeats.

Fast.

Very fast.

Dougal closed his eyes.

"Ah, no."

The hoofbeats grew louder.

There was only one person in all the Highlands stubborn enough to ride like that.

Maree Doonagan.

He turned.

A horse crested the rise behind him, charging across the moor with reckless determination. Its rider leaned low over its neck, her auburn hair whipping wildly in the wind.

Dougal muttered a prayer.

It did no good.

Maree was coming.

And she looked furious.

The horse thundered across the hillside, scattering startled birds into the evening sky. She hauled the animal to a stop so abruptly that clods of earth flew from beneath its hooves.

Before Dougal could speak, she swung from the saddle.

Stormed toward him.

And slapped him.

The crack echoed across the moor.

Dougal blinked.

The sting spread across his cheek.

For a long moment neither of them moved.

The Highlands themselves seemed to hold their breath.

Then Maree pointed a finger at his chest.

"Dougal McBeth!"

Her voice rang across the hillside.

"Ye dare leave without a goodbye? Without a reason or cause?"

The hurt in her eyes struck harder than her hand ever could.

Dougal opened his mouth.

Closed it again.

Wisely.

Maree wasn't finished.

"I'm no' like those other cheap, nasty tarts ye've conquered!"

Her voice trembled with fury and heartbreak.

"I'm a true and honest woman. I bleed this land in my veins, and ye'll no' be makin' me choose between ye and it."

The wind swept through the heather, carrying her words across the moors.

"I work this land wi' my hands. I toil in the sun and rain to make this patch o' God's earth produce guid crops. Then ye—"

She jabbed a finger toward him.

"Ye come along and mess wi' my heart only to rip it open when ye think ye've drunk o' me yer fill?"

Dougal felt every word like a blow.

Because beneath the anger lay truth.

And he knew it.

Maree took a step back.

Her eyes shone with unshed tears, but her chin remained lifted in defiance.

"I think not, Dougal McBeth."

Her voice softened.

Not weaker.

Sadder.

"I'm a Scottish lass of creed and honour, and ye... I dinna ken who or what ye are."

The words seemed to wound her as much as him.

Then came the final blow.

"But love ye I do."

The admission hung between them.

Raw.

Honest.

Terrible.

Maree swallowed hard.

"But I shall put that away now that ye're goin'."

A pause.

"Farewell, Dougal."

Without another word, she turned, mounted her horse, and rode away.

The fading sunlight caught her hair as she disappeared across the moor.

Leaving Dougal McBeth standing alone.

Stunned.

Silent.

And suddenly aware that the greatest fool in all of Scotland might just be himself.

The wind swept across the ridge.

For the first time in many years, Dougal did not look toward the road ahead.

He looked toward home.

THE AFTERMATH

Night had settled over the moors, wrapping the High-lands in darkness and shadow. The wind swept through the heather, carrying the scent of peat smoke and damp earth, while somewhere in the distance a lone owl called into the gathering gloom.

Maree Doonagan stormed toward the croft.

The slap still burned pleasantly in her palm.

The fool deserved it.

She had ridden across half the Highlands to find Dougal McBeth preparing to disappear without so much as a good-bye, and she had told him exactly what she thought of that.

And still he had left.

Her boots struck the familiar path leading home, each step fuelled by frustration. The croft stood ahead, warm light spilling from its windows, the old stone walls glowing amber against the darkness.

Doonagan stone.

Doonagan land.

Doonagan stubbornness.

Generations of her family had worked this soil. Her father had once told her that if a person listened closely enough, they could hear the voices of those who came before them carried upon the wind.

At the time she'd laughed at him.

Now she wasn't so sure.

The land remembered things.

Of that much she was certain.

She pushed open the door and stepped inside.

Warmth immediately wrapped itself around her. The scent of stew simmering on the stove mingled with the familiar smell of burning peat. The fire crackled cheerfully in the hearth.

Elspeth sat exactly where she always sat, teacup in hand, looking entirely too comfortable.

Without lifting her eyes from the cup, she asked,

"Ye've given him what for, then?"

Maree tossed her shawl onto a nearby hook.

"Aye."

Elspeth nodded.

"Good."

Maree stopped.

"Good?"

"Aye."

The old woman took another sip.

"Some men need tellin'."

Despite everything, Maree felt the corner of her mouth twitch.

It vanished quickly.

"The fool left anyway."

"Aye."

"He stood there starin' at me like a stunned sheep."

"Aye."

"I poured out me heart."

"Aye."

"I near broke me hand slappin' him."

"Aye."

Maree threw both hands into the air.

"Is that all ye've got to say?"

Elspeth finally lowered her teacup.

"What would ye like me to say, lass?"

"I'd like ye to tell me Dougal McBeth is an idiot."

The old woman considered the matter.

"Well, he is."

Maree blinked.

"That's it?"

"What more is there to say?"

The answer was so matter-of-fact that Maree couldn't help it.

She laughed.

Only for a second.

But it was enough.

The laughter disappeared as quickly as it had come.

"He left."

The words emerged quieter this time.

More honest.

The fire crackled softly between them.

Outside, the wind rattled against the stone walls.

Elspeth's expression softened.

"Aye."

Maree sank heavily into the chair opposite her.

"What is it about him?" she muttered.

The old woman raised an eyebrow.

"His thick head?"

"No."

Maree stared into the flames.

"The way he makes me forget meself."

A silence settled between them.

Not uncomfortable.

The sort of silence that belonged to old houses and older friendships.

Finally Elspeth spoke.

"He's runnin'."

Maree snorted.

"Oh, aye? And how did ye arrive at that grand conclusion?"

"Because I've eyes."

The older woman set her teacup aside.

"And because I've seen men like him before."

Maree folded her arms.

"Then tell me, wise woman. What's he runnin' from?"

"Himself."

The answer came immediately.

Maree groaned.

"That doesn't even make sense."

"It makes perfect sense."

Elspeth rose slowly and crossed toward the window.

The darkness beyond the glass stretched across the hills like a great sleeping beast.

"Some folk spend their whole lives runnin' from the very thing they're meant to become."

Maree followed her gaze.

"And Dougal's one of them?"

"Aye."

The wind howled briefly outside.

The old woman watched the distant hills.

"He's been carryin' ghosts for years."

"And ye know this how?"

"The land speaks."

Maree rolled her eyes.

"There it is."

"What?"

"Yer mysterious land talk."

Elspeth chuckled.

"Och, ye mock now, but one day ye'll understand."

The old woman rested one hand upon the windowsill.

"The rivers speak."

Maree groaned.

"The hills speak."

"Elspeth—"

"The wind speaks."

"The wind sounds like wind."

"The stones speak."

"The stones are stones."

Elspeth turned and smiled.

"And yet here ye are, listenin'."

That shut Maree up.

Because she was listening.

She always listened.

Whether she admitted it or not.

Outside, the moors stretched endlessly beneath the moonlight. Shadows moved across the hills as clouds drifted overhead.

The Highlands felt restless.

Expectant.

As though waiting for something.

Or someone.

"The Doonagans belong to this land."

Elspeth's voice had changed.

Become quieter.

More serious.

Maree frowned.

"What does that have to do with anything?"

The older woman's gaze drifted toward the darkness beyond the croft.

"A great deal."

She moved back toward the fire and settled into her chair.

"Yer father belonged to these hills."

Maree's expression softened.

"Dad always said that."

"He was right."

The old woman smiled faintly.

"So was yer grandfather."

A pause.

"And his father before him."

Maree stared into the dancing flames.

The stories came back to her then.

Stories told beside winter fires.

Stories about ancestors she'd never met.

Stories woven into the land itself.

"The Doonagans have been here a long time."

"Aye."

"Longer than most."

Elspeth nodded.

"Some roots run deeper than folk realise."

The words settled heavily between them.

For a moment Maree could almost feel those roots stretching beneath the hills and glens.

Invisible.

Ancient.

Waiting.

The feeling vanished as quickly as it came.

She shook her head.

"Ye always talk as though the land's alive."

The old woman smiled.

"What if it is?"

Maree snorted.

"Then it's as stubborn as the people livin' on it."

That earned a laugh.

A proper one.

The kind that crinkled the corners of Elspeth's eyes.

"That, lass, may be the truest thing ye've said all day."

Silence settled once more.

Comfortable.

Warm.

The fire burned steadily.

At length Elspeth spoke again.

"Dougal McBeth will return."

Maree didn't even look up.

"What makes ye so sure?"

"Because he's tied to this place now."

"And if he isn't?"

The older woman shrugged.

"Then the land will drag him back anyway."

Maree laughed despite herself.

"That's ridiculous."

"Aye."

Elspeth grinned.

"It usually is."

The younger woman shook her head.

She should have felt foolish.

Instead she felt lighter.

Not healed.

Not even close.

But steadier.

The ache remained.

The hurt remained.

Yet somewhere beneath it all was something else.

Hope.

Tiny.

Stubborn.

Refusing to die.

Perhaps Elspeth was right.

Perhaps Dougal would return.

And perhaps he wouldn't.

Either way, Maree Doonagan would endure.

She was her father's daughter.

A daughter of the Highlands.

The land had weathered storms far greater than heartbreak.

So would she.

Outside, the wind whispered across the moors.

And for the first time that night, Maree found herself listening.

GUARDIAN ELSPETH

The people of the Highlands had many stories.

Some were told beside hearth fires on winter nights.

Some were whispered over garden fences.

And some were spoken only when the wind was howling and darkness pressed against the windows.

The stories about Elspeth belonged to the last category.

No one seemed entirely certain how old she was.

Not even Elspeth.

If anyone asked, she'd simply wave a dismissive hand and say,

"Old enough to know better and young enough not to care."

Which answered absolutely nothing.

Children adored her.

Adults sought her advice.

Travellers remembered her.

And yet nobody could quite explain why.

The old croft where she lived sat upon a rise overlooking the moors, its stone walls weathered by generations of Highland storms. Smoke curled from the chimney in all seasons, and the kettle always seemed to be boiling.

People came for many reasons.

A sick child.

A broken heart.

A troublesome sheep.

An argument that refused to mend.

Elspeth dealt with all of them in much the same way.

With tea.

And honesty.

Usually in that order.

On this particular morning, a young shepherd named Hamish MacLaren arrived at her door looking thoroughly miserable.

Elspeth took one glance at him and sighed.

"What have ye broken now?"

Hamish blinked.

"How did ye ken I'd broken somethin'?"

"Because ye've got the expression of a man who's either broken somethin' or married the wrong woman."

The young man looked relieved.

"Just a fence."

"Good."

Elspeth ushered him inside.

"A fence is easier to repair."

The shepherd laughed despite himself.

Within minutes he was seated beside the fire, clutching a mug of tea while Elspeth listened to his tale of wandering sheep and collapsing stone walls.

When he finally finished, she nodded.

"Then rebuild the fence."

Hamish stared at her.

"That's yer advice?"

"Aye."

"But what if it falls down again?"

Elspeth shrugged.

"Then ye rebuild it again."

The young man frowned.

"That seems overly simple."

"Och, Hamish. Most problems are."

By the time he left, he was smiling.

The fence, Elspeth suspected, would survive.

The same could not be said for his sheep.

The morning passed quietly after that.

The wind moved through the heather beyond the croft.

The hills stretched beneath a sky of drifting cloud.

Everything appeared ordinary.

But appearances had never impressed Elspeth.

The Highlands were rarely as quiet as they seemed.

She stepped outside carrying a basket of herbs.

The moment her boots touched the earth, she paused.

Something felt different.

A subtle shift.

The sort of thing most people missed.

The wind changed direction.

A raven called from somewhere beyond the ridge.

The hairs on the back of her neck stirred.

Elspeth looked toward the distant hills.

"Hmph."

The land was restless again.

Not dangerous.

Not yet.

Simply awake.

She continued gathering herbs, though her attention remained fixed upon the horizon.

Far below, she spotted Maree crossing one of the lower fields.

Even at a distance the girl moved with purpose.

Strong.

Determined.

Rooted.

A Doonagan through and through.

Elspeth smiled faintly.

The lass had no idea what lay ahead.

None of them did.

Not Maree.

Not Isla.

Not Fergus.

Not Caitriona.

Not even Ewan.

Scattered branches of the same family tree.

Each living their own lives.

Each believing they had chosen their own paths.

The old woman shook her head.

Life was rarely that simple.

The Highlands had a way of gathering its own.

Sooner or later.

The wind stirred again.

This time carrying the faint scent of rain.

Elspeth turned toward the standing stones visible on the distant rise.

Ancient sentinels.

Silent witnesses.

Older than memory.

For a moment she studied them.

Then she smiled.

"Patience."

The word vanished into the breeze.

A stranger watching might have thought she was speaking to herself.

Perhaps she was.

Or perhaps she wasn't.

The Highlands kept their secrets.

And Elspeth had learned long ago that some mysteries revealed themselves only when the time was right.

The afternoon sun drifted westward.

The hills glowed gold.

Somewhere beyond the horizon, lives were shifting.

Choices were being made.

Journeys were beginning.

The old woman could feel it.

Not because she possessed any special gift.

At least, that was what she told people.

But because after a lifetime spent listening, she had learned something important.

The land always knew before anyone else.

And the land was listening now.

As evening settled across the moors, Elspeth stood alone outside her croft.

The wind tugged gently at her silver hair.

The standing stones watched from afar.

The Highlands waited.

And deep beneath the hills, beneath the roots of ancient trees and the bones of forgotten generations, something long asleep stirred.

Elspeth's smile faded.

"About time."

The wind swept across the moors.

And somewhere beyond the gathering darkness, destiny took its first step toward home.

MAREE'S RESOLVE

The following morning dawned clear and bright across the Highlands.

Golden sunlight spilled across the moors, turning the dew-covered heather into a sea of sparkling silver and gold. A skylark rose from the grass, its song drifting across the hills as though welcoming the day.

Maree Doonagan stepped from the croft and inhaled deeply.

The air carried the familiar scents of damp earth, peat smoke, and heather.

Home.

The word settled comfortably within her.

No matter how much the world changed, the Highlands remained.

The hills remained.

The land remained.

And so did she.

A soft nicker came from the paddock.

Her Highland mare watched her expectantly.

"Aye, aye," Maree said. "I'm comin'."

The horse snorted.

Maree narrowed her eyes.

"Ye've got opinions this mornin', haven't ye?"

The mare nudged the fence.

"Well, keep them to yerself."

The horse ignored her.

Maree smiled despite herself.

Animals had a remarkable ability to put life into perspective.

They didn't care about broken hearts.

They cared about breakfast.

The chickens were equally demanding.

By the time Maree reached the coop, they were already voicing their complaints.

"Ye'd think I starved the lot o' ye."

The hens disagreed loudly.

She scattered grain and watched them descend into chaos.

Life continued.

It always did.

The realization brought a strange comfort.

The world had not ended because Dougal McBeth had ridden away.

The sun still rose.

The hens still squabbled.

The hills still stood.

And she still had work to do.

A familiar voice drifted from behind her.

"Talkin' to chickens again?"

Maree didn't turn.

"They listen better than people."

Elspeth chuckled.

"That's because chickens have more sense than most people."

"Especially men."

"Aye."

The old woman moved to stand beside her.

"Particularly men."

Together they watched the hens for a moment.

The silence between them was easy.

Comfortable.

Like a well-worn blanket.

The sort that came only from years of knowing one another.

Maree rested her arms upon the fence.

The morning sun warmed her face.

Beyond the fields, the moors stretched endlessly toward the distant hills.

The sight stirred memories.

Her father loved mornings like this.

Duncan Doonagan had always risen before the sun.

As a child, Maree would stumble sleepily into the fields and find him already working.

He'd straighten from whatever task occupied him and grin beneath his fiery beard.

"Come to inspect me work, have ye?"

She smiled at the memory.

Duncan never simply worked the land.

He loved it.

Every stone wall.

Every field.

Every stubborn sheep.

Every patch of heather.

"The land gives back what ye give it, lass," he'd often tell her.

At the time she'd thought he was speaking about farming.

Now she suspected he'd meant something far deeper.

Arabella understood it too.

Though in a different way.

Where Duncan saw the practical side of the Highlands, Arabella saw the stories.

Winter evenings had belonged to her mother.

Firelight dancing across the walls.

A knitting basket beside her chair.

Ancient tales flowing as naturally as breathing.

Stories of clans.

Stories of courage.

Stories of love and sacrifice.

Stories that seemed woven into the very hills surrounding them.

Maree could still hear her voice sometimes.

Not clearly.

Not as a sound.

More as a memory carried upon the wind.

The ache never truly disappeared.

Years had passed since illness had stolen both her parents.

Yet there were mornings when the loss felt as fresh as yesterday.

"They'd be proud o' ye."

Elspeth's voice broke gently into her thoughts.

Maree blinked.

"Ye dinnae know that."

"I do."

The old woman sounded utterly certain.

"Duncan would burst with pride every time ye argued with somebody."

Maree laughed.

"That's probably true."

"And Arabella?"

Elspeth smiled.

"She always knew ye'd stay."

The words settled heavily upon her.

Because they were true.

Her siblings had each followed different roads.

Ewan carried his own responsibilities now.

Isla chased music wherever it led.

Fergus followed horizons most folk never saw.

And Caitriona pursued learning with the same determination other people reserved for treasure.

Each had found their own path.

But Maree had remained.

Not because she lacked choices.

Because she had made one.

The croft.

The land.

The legacy.

The Doonagans.

Someone had to remember.

Someone had to remain.

The realization surprised her.

She had always viewed staying as duty.

Now it felt like something else.

A calling.

Elspeth seemed to sense the shift.

"Yer father understood."

"Understood what?"

"That belonging is a gift."

The old woman gestured toward the hills.

"Most spend their lives searching for where they fit."

Maree followed her gaze.

The Highlands rolled endlessly into the distance.

Wild.

Ancient.

Beautiful.

"This is where ye belong."

The statement should have felt obvious.

Instead it felt profound.

Because for the first time in weeks, perhaps months, she wasn't thinking about Dougal.

She wasn't wondering where he was.

Or what he was doing.

Or whether he'd return.

She was simply standing upon her land.

Breathing Highland air.

Feeling the strength of generations beneath her feet.

And somehow that was enough.

At least for today.

The wind swept across the moors.

Carrying the scent of heather and distant rain.

Maree lifted her face toward it.

For a fleeting moment she thought she heard something hidden within the breeze.

A whisper.

A memory.

A promise.

Then it was gone.

She smiled.

Perhaps Elspeth was rubbing off on her after all.

The old woman raised an eyebrow.

"What are ye grinnin' at?"

Maree shook her head.

"Nothin'."

Elspeth looked unconvinced.

But she let it go.

Together they stood watching the Highlands awaken beneath the morning sun.

And deep within her heart, Maree felt something settling into place.

Not happiness.

Not yet.

Something stronger.

Resolve.

Whatever the future held, she would meet it as a Doonagan.

As her father's daughter.

As her mother's child.

As a woman of the Highlands.

And for now, that was enough.

CHAPTER 5

DOUGAL'S REFLECTION

The moors stretched endlessly before him.

Heather rippled beneath the morning wind, flowing like a purple sea across the Highland hills. Mist lingered in the valleys below, slowly surrendering to the rising sun.

Dougal McBeth walked without purpose.

Or at least that was what he told himself.

His boots followed an old track winding through the hills, though he could not remember consciously choosing it.

Maree's voice still echoed in his mind.

Sharp.

Honest.

Painfully deserved.

He could still feel the sting of her hand against his cheek.

Not because it hurt.

Because it mattered.

Nobody had ever ridden across half the Highlands to stop him leaving before.

Most simply watched him go.

The wind pressed against him.

Cold.

Insistent.

As though urging him onward.

Or perhaps urging him back.

He wasn't sure which.

That uncertainty irritated him.

For most of his life, moving on had been easy.

Necessary.

The moment a place began to feel comfortable, he left.

The moment roots threatened to grow, he moved.

It was safer that way.

Safer than disappointment.

Safer than failure.

Safer than becoming his father.

His jaw tightened.

The old man had cast a long shadow.

Even now.

Especially now.

Dougal reached down and brushed his fingers through the heather as he walked.

The scent rose immediately.

Wild.

Familiar.

Ancient.

Something about these hills unsettled him.

Not because they were unfamiliar.

Because they weren't.

And that made no sense.

He had never truly belonged anywhere.

Had he?

A memory surfaced unexpectedly.

Rain battered the windows of their small cottage while his father sat beside the fire mending a broken harness.

The old man rarely spoke.

Yet every now and then, usually after a dram or two, old memories seemed to slip through cracks he spent the rest of his life trying to seal shut.

There had been stories.

Fragments.

Half-finished conversations.

Never enough to form a complete picture.

Only enough to leave questions.

One name appeared more than once.

Clachanoch.

Even now, the word stirred something within him.

Not recognition.

Not exactly.

Something deeper.

Something older.

He remembered asking his father about it when he was a boy.

The old man's face had changed immediately.

The conversation ended before it truly began.

Dougal never forgot that.

Nor did he forget the faded journal he had once discovered hidden among his father's belongings.

Most of it had been damaged by time.

Yet inside were rough sketches of a great stone house standing proudly against the Highlands.

Tall windows.

Sweeping grounds.

An estate built to endure.

And beneath one sketch, written in faded ink, was a single word.

Clachanoch.

His father had snatched the journal away before Dougal could ask more.

The memory still lingered.

As did the questions.

The wind stirred again.

Dougal frowned.

Strange.

For years he had dismissed those fragments.

Told himself they didn't matter.

Yet lately the name returned more often.

Clachanoch.

A whisper at the edge of thought.

A half-remembered melody.

A mystery that refused to remain buried.

He shook his head.

Ridiculous.

Probably an old estate.

A family connection long since lost.

Nothing more.

And yet...

The feeling persisted.

His boots carried him higher onto the ridge until he reached a rocky outcrop overlooking the surrounding countryside.

Dougal lowered himself onto the stone.

Below him, the Highlands unfolded in every direction.

Ancient hills.

Winding rivers.

Stone walls tracing forgotten boundaries.

The landscape seemed eternal.

Unchanging.

For a long moment he simply sat.

Listening.

The wind moved through the heather.

A raven called somewhere overhead.

Far in the distance sunlight touched the upper slopes of a hill.

And for reasons he couldn't explain, Dougal felt something shift within him.

A sense of belonging.

Brief.

Unexpected.

Gone almost immediately.

Yet powerful enough to leave him unsettled.

Home.

The word arrived uninvited.

Home.

He almost laughed.

The idea was absurd.

Home belonged to people like Maree.

People with roots.

Families.

Land.

People who knew where they belonged.

Not men who wandered from one season to the next carrying little more than a trade and a pack.

His hands turned over slowly in his lap.

Strong hands.

Scarred hands.

Woodworker's hands.

The only thing he had ever truly mastered.

Wood made sense.

Wood could be shaped.

Given purpose.

Given form.

People were far more complicated.

Especially women with fiery tempers and brave hearts.

A reluctant smile touched his lips.

Maree.

She had demanded honesty.

Nothing more.

Nothing less.

And somehow that had frightened him more than anything else.

Because honesty required staying.

The wind rose again.

This time carrying the scent of distant rain.

Dougal stood.

Far below, the road stretched toward the croft.

Toward Maree.

Toward choices he had spent years avoiding.

For the first time, the thought of returning did not feel like surrender.

It felt like courage.

He looked once more across the Highlands.

The hills stood silent.

Watching.

Waiting.

And somewhere deep within him, a forgotten mystery stirred once more.

Clachanoch.

Though he could not have explained why, Dougal suddenly felt certain of one thing.

His journey was not taking him away from something.

It was leading him toward it.

CROFT REUNION

The Highland wind carried more than the scent of heather that evening.

It carried change.

Dougal McBeth stood at the edge of the croft, staring at the familiar stone walls bathed in the golden light of sunset. Smoke curled lazily from the chimney, drifting across the moors before disappearing into the gathering dusk.

For a long moment, he simply stood there.

The croft looked exactly the same.

Yet nothing felt the same.

His stomach tightened.

He had faced storms, difficult employers, angry landowners, and hardships across half of Scotland.

None of them frightened him half as much as knocking on this door.

Because Maree was on the other side.

And this time, he had no intention of running.

Drawing a steadying breath, he crossed the yard and knocked.

Almost immediately, the door swung open.

Maree stood there.

A dusting of flour marked one cheek. Strands of auburn hair had escaped whatever attempt she'd made to tame them. Her sleeves were rolled up, and she looked as though she'd spent the entire day working.

She was beautiful.

The thought struck him so suddenly he nearly forgot why he'd come.

For several heartbeats neither of them spoke.

Then Maree folded her arms.

"Ye came back."

Not relief.

Not accusation.

Simply fact.

"Aye."

Her eyes narrowed slightly.

"Took ye long enough."

Dougal almost smiled.

Almost.

"Fair."

Maree studied him.

The wind stirred between them.

Finally she stepped aside.

"Well? Are ye standin' there all night?"

He blinked.

"Does that mean I can come in?"

"It means if ye keep lettin' all the warm air out, I'll regret opening the door."

Dougal stepped inside.

The familiar warmth wrapped around him immediately.

The scent of baking bread filled the room.

The fire crackled softly in the hearth.

Everything about the croft felt welcoming.

Everything except the woman standing before him.

Not hostile.

Just cautious.

As she should be.

Maree returned to the table where dough waited beneath a cloth.

She resumed kneading.

With considerable force.

Dougal wisely remained standing.

For now.

The silence stretched.

Eventually Maree spoke.

"What changed?"

The question was simple.

The answer wasn't.

Dougal looked toward the fire.

Then back at her.

"I got tired."

"Tired?"

"Aye."

"Of what?"

He hesitated.

"Running."

Her hands slowed.

Only slightly.

But he noticed.

"I've spent years leavin' places before they could matter."

Maree said nothing.

So he continued.

"I told maself it was freedom."

The fire popped softly.

"But truth is, it was fear."

Now her hands stopped entirely.

For the first time since he'd arrived, she looked directly at him.

Fear.

Not many men admitted such things.

Especially Highland men.

Dougal swallowed.

"I thought if I never stayed long enough to care, I'd never have anything to lose."

Maree lowered her gaze.

"And how did that work out for ye?"

A humourless laugh escaped him.

"Poorly."

That earned the faintest twitch at the corner of her mouth.

A victory.

Small.

But real.

He moved closer to the table.

Not enough to crowd her.

Just enough to show he wasn't leaving.

"I was wrong, Maree."

The words hung in the air.

Simple.

Honest.

"No excuses."

She looked up.

"No grand speeches?"

"Nae."

"No dramatic declarations?"

"Not unless ye insist."

That earned an unwilling snort.

She immediately looked annoyed with herself.

Dougal smiled.

The first genuine smile since arriving.

Maree pointed a flour-covered finger at him.

"Dinnae get comfortable."

"Aye, lass."

Silence settled again.

But this time it felt different.

Less sharp.

Less brittle.

Maree resumed kneading.

More gently now.

Eventually she spoke.

"Ye hurt me."

The words landed harder than any slap.

"I know."

"I waited."

His chest tightened.

"I know."

"I made excuses for ye."

Every word carried quiet truth.

"I know."

Maree blinked rapidly and looked away.

For the first time since his return, Dougal saw the hurt beneath the anger.

The disappointment.

The uncertainty.

The loneliness.

And suddenly he hated himself for causing it.

"I canna change what I did."

"No."

"But I'd like the chance tae do better."

The room fell silent.

Only the fire spoke.

Outside, the wind rattled gently against the stone walls.

Finally Maree sighed.

A long, weary sigh.

The sort carried by people who were tired of fighting.

"I'm still angry."

"Fair."

"I'm no' entirely convinced ye've grown a brain."

"Also fair."

"And if ye disappear again—"

"I won't."

She fixed him with a look.

"If ye disappear again, Dougal McBeth, I'll hunt ye down."

A smile tugged at his lips.

"Aye, ye probably will."

The door suddenly burst open.

Elspeth entered carrying a basket.

She stopped.

Looked at Maree.

Looked at Dougal.

Looked back at Maree.

Then sighed dramatically.

"Oh good."

Neither of them spoke.

Elspeth set the basket down.

"I was worried one of ye might do somethin' sensible and ruin all the entertainment."

Maree groaned.

"Elspeth."

"What?"

The old woman looked entirely innocent.

"I've spent weeks listenin' tae the pair of ye pine after each other."

"We have not."

"Oh, aye?"

Elspeth raised an eyebrow.

"Then perhaps I imagined all the sighing."

Dougal coughed into his hand.

Maree threw a dish towel at him.

Traitor.

The old woman grinned.

Satisfied that disaster had been avoided, she moved toward the hearth.

"Well."

She settled into her chair.

"Carry on."

"Carry on with what?" Maree demanded.

Elspeth waved a hand.

"Whatever this is."

Maree buried her face in her hands.

Dougal laughed.

Properly laughed.

And for the first time in what felt like forever, Maree laughed too.

Not because everything was fixed.

Not because all wounds had healed.

But because hope had returned.

Later, after Elspeth finally stopped meddling and the bread had been baked, Dougal stood outside beneath a sky scattered with stars.

Maree joined him.

Neither spoke immediately.

The moors stretched away beneath the moonlight.

Ancient.

Patient.

Enduring.

Much like the woman beside him.

After a while, Maree slipped her hand into his.

Not forgiveness.

Not yet.

Not entirely.

But trust.

A beginning.

A promise.

Dougal closed his fingers gently around hers.

And together they stood beneath the Highland sky, watching the stars emerge one by one, unaware that far greater journeys awaited them both.

For now, it was enough that neither of them stood alone.

SECRETS UNVEILED

The morning stretched long over the moors, sunlight spilling in soft ribbons across the heather. The scent of damp earth and woodsmoke clung to the air as Maree and Dougal worked side by side, their hands busy with the demands of the croft.

Maree, sleeves rolled to her elbows, was stacking the last of the stones along the paddock wall, while Dougal split logs with an easy rhythm, each swing of the axe sharp and precise.

They had fallen into an unspoken truce over the past few days—working together, sharing meals, speaking in measured exchanges. But beneath it, something still simmered. Something neither of them dared name just yet.

The rhythm of their labour was almost comfortable—almost. But now and then, Maree would glance sideways when she thought he wasn't looking. And Dougal, pausing to wipe his brow, would let his gaze linger on her profile longer than sense permitted. There was something in the way they moved—apart, but always returning to each other, like waves circling a tide-worn shore.

"Ye've done this before," Maree remarked, dusting off her hands.

Dougal nodded, adjusting his grip on the axe. "Aye. Spent time on crofts now and then. Good, honest work. But it was never mine."

Maree studied him. "And what was?"

He set the axe aside, leaning against the fence post. "Woodturnin'."

She arched a brow. "Aye?"

"Aye." His gaze drifted toward the croft's barn, as if he could see the old lathe within. "There's a satisfaction in shapin' wood—takin' a rough, stubborn bit o' timber and coaxin' somethin' fine out of it. A chair, a spindle, a bannock board... even just a simple bowl. There's a patience to it." He glanced at her. "Ye have to work with the grain, not against it."

Maree crossed her arms, lips twitching. "A rare thought for a man who's spent his life fightin' against things."

Dougal huffed a quiet laugh. "Aye, well. Took me a long time to see it that way."

Maree turned toward the chicken coop, tossing a handful of grain into the dirt. "And what else did ye see out there, on yer travels?"

Dougal leaned against the paddock, folding his arms as he thought.

"I've stood beneath the Northern Lights," he said, voice quieter now. "Watched the sky ripple in green and blue over the fjords, silent as breath. Thought for a moment I'd wandered into some other world."

Maree paused, captivated despite herself.

"I've walked the markets in Marrakech," he continued, "where the air is thick wi' spice and the air hums wi' voices from every corner o' the world. I learned to barter in a dozen tongues, though I never had much worth tradin'." He smiled, remembering. "Met a man there, an old woodworker, who could carve a camel from a scrap o' cedar wi' nothin' but a pocket knife. He laughed when I told him I was a woodturner, said I had the hands for it, but not the patience."

Maree huffed a soft laugh. "A wise man, then."

Dougal smirked. "Aye. But he taught me a few tricks, all the same."

He hesitated before going on.

"I've seen the great deserts in the East, stood atop the dunes as the sun turned the sand to gold. There's a silence there, Maree—no wind, no birds, just the weight o' the sky pressin' down on ye. Thought I might disappear into it, once or twice."

She frowned, studying him. "And did ye want to?"

Dougal exhaled, running a hand through his hair. "Aye. Maybe. There's a freedom in belongin' to nothin'."

Maree nodded slowly. "But it doesn't last."

He met her gaze, something shifting between them. "No. It doesn't."

Silence settled, thick and charged.

A breeze stirred between them, lifting Maree's hair and curling the scent of hearth smoke around them. It was as if the moors had leaned in, quieting the world to make room for this fragile moment, this truth long buried beneath pride and fear.

Then Maree reached out, catching his hand in hers. It was a small thing, calloused fingers curling around calloused fingers, but Dougal felt it like an anchor.

"I dinnae ken much about deserts or far-off markets," she murmured. "But I ken what it is to feel untethered. To lose somethin' and not be sure if ye'll ever find it again."

Dougal's throat tightened. He turned his palm, his thumb brushing over the rough skin of hers.

"Maree—"

She stepped closer, just a breath between them now. "Just hush for a moment."

Then she kissed him.

It wasn't rushed, nor uncertain. It was slow, deliberate—like the turn of a chisel against wood, shaping something new.

The kiss settled between them like a stone in water, soft, but sending ripples deep. Her lips were warm, firm, sure. And when he responded, it wasn't with the hesitance of a man returning—it was with the certainty of a man arriving.

Dougal inhaled sharply, his hands settling gently at her waist. The warmth of her, the scent of her—heather and fresh bread, earth and rain—wrapped around him, grounding him in a way nothing ever had before.

Maree's fingers traced the line of his jaw before she pulled back, eyes searching his. "Dinnae leave again," she whispered.

He cupped the side of her face, brushing his thumb over her cheek. "I won't."

For a moment, neither of them moved.

Then Maree smirked. "If I'd known kissin' ye would get ye to finally shut up, I'd have done it sooner."

Dougal laughed, the sound warm and easy. "Aye, well, I'd no be opposed to a bit more hushin'."

Maree huffed, swatting him lightly on the chest before stepping back toward the croft. "Come on, then. I want to see if ye can actually work that lathe, or if ye're all talk."

Dougal grinned, rolling up his sleeves. "Aye, lass. We'll see soon enough."

And as he followed her toward the barn, something settled deep in his chest—something that told him, at long last, he'd found his place.

Elspeth had watched the pair from the doorway, her keen eyes missing nothing. She had seen the way Maree had softened, how Dougal had steadied. She had seen the way they moved together—not just in work, but in something deeper, something unspoken.

She stepped out a little farther, her shadow stretching long across the path. The land had shifted again—she could feel it in her knees, in the whisper that rustled through the gorse. Change had come, not with thunder or fanfare, but with two stubborn hearts finally letting go.

The moors had a way of shaping people, just as surely as the wind carved the cliffs and the rain softened the earth. They did not rush, nor bend easily. But when they found their course, they endured.

Maree and Dougal were like that.

She smiled to herself, stepping back into the croft, letting them have their moment. The moors had witnessed many stories, but this one—this one had a heartbeat all its own.

And as the wind swept across the land, it carried with it the quiet murmur of something ancient and true.

Home.

STORM OF LOVE AND GALES

The Highland sky, once adorned with a tapestry of stars, had turned black with storm clouds, heavy with the weight of impending rain. The air thickened, charged with something more than just the coming tempest—it was as though the land itself could feel the quiet storm brewing within the walls of the croft.

The first drops of rain struck the earth in a slow, deliberate rhythm, but within moments, the heavens broke open, releasing a wild torrent. The wind howled through the moors, rattling the shutters, shaking the very bones of the croft.

Inside, Maree and Dougal stood near the hearth, the flickering light of the fire dancing over their faces. The storm outside had mirrored something between them—something they had danced around for too long.

The flames snapped and swirled, casting shadows that seemed to pulse with the wind's cry. Maree's breath came short, her thoughts loud in the silence between them. Every instinct screamed that something was about to shift, like standing on a cliff edge just before the earth gives way.

Maree, arms wrapped around herself, stared into the flames, the glow casting golden hues across her skin. "I can feel it, Dougal," she murmured, voice barely above the wind's wail. "This... between us. The storm's dragged it to the surface, and now I cannae push it back down."

Dougal exhaled, raking a hand through his hair. "Aye, I feel it too." He turned toward the window, watching as the rain lashed against the glass. "I've spent my whole life runnin'—from places, from people, from anything that could hold me. And yet... when I left here, it felt like I was leavin' somethin' I should never have walked away from."

Maree swallowed hard. "And what is that?"

Dougal turned to her then, his eyes dark with something deep and unshaken. "You, Maree."

The words struck her like thunder in her chest. She had thought she was prepared for this, for whatever feelings had been stirring between them, but to hear it—to know it—sent a shiver through her that had nothing to do with the cold.

"I love ye," Dougal said, the confession rough and unpolished, but fierce with truth. "I love ye in a way I never expected to love anyone. It terrifies me, but I cannae change it. I cannae fight it." He took a step closer, his voice lower now, almost lost beneath the howling wind. "I don't want to fight it."

Maree's breath caught, her hands curling into fists as she tried to steady herself against the whirlwind of emotions crashing over her. She had spent so long guarding her heart, tending the land, believing she needed nothing more than the soil beneath her feet and the sky above her head. But Dougal had unsettled something in her—something deep, something she had feared giving voice to.

And yet, there it was.

"I love ye too," she whispered.

The storm raged, the fire crackled, and between them, something broke—something old, something unspoken.

Dougal reached for her, his hands warm and calloused as they cradled her face. "Say it again," he murmured, as if he couldn't quite believe it.

Maree let out a breathless laugh, tilting her chin defiantly. "I love ye, Dougal McBeth. And if ye ever leave me again, I'll make sure ye regret it."

He chuckled, but there was something raw in the way he looked at her, something aching. "I willnae leave, Maree. Not ever again."

And then he kissed her.

It was slow at first, tentative, like the first roll of thunder before the storm breaks. But then it deepened, all the tension and longing of the past weeks, months, years—pouring into that single moment. His arms wrapped around her, pulling her against him, and she melted into his embrace, letting the warmth of him chase away the lingering chill.

Their kiss didn't feel like an end or even a beginning—it felt like the moment the rain hits dry earth, the long-awaited answer to an aching drought. They had survived the storm before the storm. Now, they simply held each other, hearts thudding in time with the tempest.

The wind screamed against the croft, rain hammering at the roof, but inside, they were safe. Inside, there was only the fire, the touch of his hands, the way his lips moved against hers as if he had waited a lifetime to do this.

A sudden crack of lightning split the sky, the flash illuminating the room in a stark, electric glow. Maree gasped as the power of it trembled through the walls, breaking them apart from their trance.

And then, from the shadows, a voice.

"Well, it's about bloody time."

They broke apart, breathless, to find Elspeth standing in the doorway, arms crossed over her chest, a knowing smirk on her lips.

Maree groaned, covering her face with her hands. "Elspeth—"

The old woman waved a hand. "Och, dinnae start wi' me. Ye two have been circlin' each other like a pair o' daft birds for long enough." She stepped closer, eyeing them both with an expression that was equal parts mischief and something older, something wiser.

She gestured toward the storm outside. "The land, the sky, the very wind—they all carry stories. The storms come and they go, but they always leave things changed. It's the same wi' love." She eyed Dougal with a sharpness that cut through the warmth of the moment. "And love, lad, is no' just somethin' ye say. It's somethin' ye do. Every day. Every choice. Are ye ready for that?"

Dougal met her gaze, his hold on Maree tightening just slightly. "Aye. I am."

Elspeth nodded, satisfied. "Good. Because this lass deserves more than just words."

The old woman's gaze softened, and for a brief moment, something like pride flickered across her face. Not the loud sort, but the kind that settles deep in the bones of those who've waited a long time to see a promise kept.

Maree swallowed the lump in her throat. She wanted to roll her eyes, to quip back, to deflect—but there was no hiding from Elspeth's wisdom.

The older woman turned, moving toward the fire, settling herself into her chair as if she had not just walked into the most private moment of their lives.

Maree, cheeks still warm, glanced up at Dougal. He was watching her, something soft in his expression, something steady.

She squeezed his hand.

The storm outside still raged, but within the croft, a different kind of storm had settled—one that had left them standing not apart, but together.

And for the first time, Maree knew she would never have to weather another alone.

NEW BEGINNINGS

A s dawn broke over the Highlands, the storm that had raged through the night finally relented. The moors, once beaten down by wind and rain, now glistened with fresh dew, the scent of wet earth and heather rising with the morning sun.

Maree stepped outside first, boots sinking into the damp grass, her breath curling in the crisp air. Dougal followed, stretching out his arms as though shaking off the remnants of the tempest. The croft had endured, standing strong against the wind's fury, just as they had.

A moment of silence settled between them as they took in the transformed landscape.

"The moors have a way o' washin' away the clutter o' the past, don't they?" Dougal finally said, his voice quiet but sure.

Maree exhaled, a small smile tugging at her lips. "Aye, like a fresh start. A clean slate." She turned to him then, eyes steady. "It's time we talk, Dougal—about us. And what comes next."

They walked toward the paddock, hands brushing but not quite clasping, the unspoken still lingering in the cool air.

"I ken I've been wanderin', Maree," Dougal admitted, glancing toward the distant hills. "But it's different now. I want to build somethin' here. With ye. If ye'll have me."

Maree studied him, reading the truth in his face. She had always been tethered to this land, her roots buried deep in the croft's soil. But Dougal had always been the wind, untamed and uncertain. And yet, here he was, offering something solid.

"I've cherished this croft, Dougal," she said softly. "And I've come to cherish ye. But we need to understand each other—our dreams, our fears—if this is goin' to work."

Dougal nodded, reaching for her hand, this time fully clasping it. "Aye, lass. We'll figure it out together."

A shared commitment settled between them, not just to each other, but to a future neither had expected.

From behind them, a familiar voice cut through the quiet morning.

"Ah, well, that's settled then. Ye're no' daft after all."

They turned to find Elspeth, standing by the stone wall, arms crossed, smirking like a cat who'd just knocked over the cream jug.

Maree groaned. "Elspeth, how long have ye been listenin'?"

The old woman shrugged. "Long enough. Ye two have been dancin' around each other like spooked foals. Took a storm to knock some sense into ye, aye?"

Dougal huffed a laugh, but Maree narrowed her eyes. "And what are ye doin' out here so early?"

Elspeth lifted her chin, eyes twinkling with mischief. "Celebratin', of course."

And before they could ask what exactly she meant by that, she bolted straight into the open moor, arms spread wide, skirts flying, laughing as she spun beneath the golden light of morning.

Dougal blinked. "What in the—?"

"She's lost her mind," Maree muttered, pinching the bridge of her nose.

Elspeth twirled through the damp grass, lifting her hands to the sky. "Ahh, the air is fresh, the storm has passed, and love is in bloom! The very hills are singin' this day!"

Maree planted her hands on her hips. "Elspeth, get back here before ye slip and break a hip!"

"Break a hip?" Elspeth scoffed, pausing long enough to shoot Maree a scandalised look. "Lass, I've climbed more hills than ye've had breakfasts. My bones may be old, but they're not brittle."

With that, she kicked off her shoes and sprinted barefoot through the moors.

Dougal grinned. "Should we be stoppin' her, or...?"

Maree sighed, but even she couldn't keep the smirk from forming. "Och, let her be. She's daft as they come, but... she's right."

Dougal tugged her toward him. "About the dancin' or about us?"

Maree tipped her head up, her blue eyes meeting his. "Both."

He kissed her then, slow and deep, the warmth of it sinking into her bones. When they pulled apart, the moors felt quieter somehow, as if the land itself had settled into the moment with them.

Elspeth, still twirling nearby, suddenly whooped. "Aye! Now that's how ye do it!"

Dougal laughed against Maree's temple. "Ye think if we ignore her, she'll get tired?"

Maree snorted. "Not likely. But let's try anyway."

They turned back toward the croft, hand in hand, the moors stretching wide before them, open and full of possibility.

But just as they reached the door, something—or rather, someone—caught their eye.

A lone figure stood on the ridge, the wind tugging at his dark coat. His stance was one of a man who had travelled far and seen much, but there was something unmistakably familiar about him.

For a moment, even the wind seemed to hush, curling around the stranger as if trying to place him back in the folds of the land where he once belonged.

Maree narrowed her eyes. "Who's that?"

Dougal frowned, shading his eyes against the sun. Then his breath hitched. "Angus."

Maree glanced at him. "Ye ken him?"

"Aye," Dougal murmured, something unreadable in his tone. "He's kin. And it looks like he's finally come home."

A soft gust passed over the ridge, bending the heather as if bowing to a returning soul. The moors, ever watchful, seemed to draw a quiet breath.

The wind shifted, carrying the scent of rain and heather, and with it, the promise of new beginnings—for all of them.

ARRIVAL OF NEW FACES

By the time Angus reached them, he was smiling. Not the hesitant smile of a man uncertain of his welcome, but the warm, lopsided grin of kin returning home, even if he wasn't sure where home truly was.

"Dougal McBeth," he said, stopping a few paces away. "As I live and breathe."

Dougal's face split into a grin as he closed the distance in two strides, pulling Angus into a rough embrace, clapping him hard on the back.

"Ye mad wanderer! What in blazes are ye doin' here?"

Angus laughed. "Ach, heard word in the next village that a certain McBeth had stopped runnin'. Thought I'd see it with me own eyes."

Dougal stepped back, still grinning. "And?"

Angus looked around, taking in the croft, the land, the woman standing beside his cousin. His eyes held something thoughtful, something knowing. "Aye. Seems they weren't lyin'."

The wind lifted a strand of Maree's hair, carrying it across her cheek like a blessing from the hills themselves. She tucked it behind her ear, never breaking eye contact with the newcomer. There was something in Angus's presence that stirred her curiosity—not in the way Dougal had unsettled her, but in the way a sudden weather shift might make a farmer pause mid-harvest.

Maree folded her arms, studying him. He was a man built for travel, that much was clear. Stocky, strong, with the sort of quiet resilience that came from years of surviving on wits and will alone. His dark-blonde hair was streaked with grey, not from age but from time spent beneath the punishing South American sun. And his eyes, deep-set and bright with the knowledge of lands far beyond Scotland, they held stories.

"And ye are?" Angus asked, turning his gaze to her.

"Maree Doonagan," she replied. "Owner of this croft. And Dougal's the one who had to prove he was worth the land."

Angus's mouth quirked. "Did he pass?"

Maree shrugged, but her lips twitched. "Jury's still out."

Angus chuckled. "Well, I like ye already."

Dougal shook his head, gesturing toward the croft. "Come in, man. There's stew on the fire, and whisky enough for stories."

Angus followed without hesitation, as though he had always been meant to cross this threshold.

Inside, the warmth of the hearth drove away the last traces of the storm's chill. Angus shed his coat, settling into a chair by the fire like a man who had spent a lifetime sitting by different hearths, never quite claiming one as his own.

The fire snapped gently, casting amber light across the floorboards, and the smell of barley stew thickened the air with comfort. The croft seemed to welcome Angus without question, its old bones creaking softly in the wind like a house that knew how to embrace strangers.

Maree set out another bowl as Dougal poured whisky, and soon they were seated, the glow of the fire casting flickering light over Angus's weathered face.

"So," Dougal said, leaning forward, "tell me, cousin. Where have ye been?"

Angus exhaled, swirling the whisky in his glass. "Everywhere."

He glanced toward the flames, his gaze distant for a moment, as though he could see the places he had walked reflected in the embers.

"I've stood in the markets of Cusco, where the air is thick wi' spice and the streets are a riot of colour. I've walked the edges of the Atacama, where the ground's so dry, it's as if time itself forgot to pass through it. And I've lived beneath the canopy of the Amazon, where the river moves like a great, breathin' thing, and the trees whisper secrets to those who know how to listen."

Maree, spoon paused halfway to her mouth, stared at him. "And why leave all that?"

Angus hesitated, but only for a second. Then he smiled, lifting his glass. "Because even the wildest rivers lead somewhere."

There was a faint wistfulness in his voice—something Maree couldn't quite place. Not sadness, not regret. More like the tug of a chapter closing behind him.

Dougal clinked his glass against his. "And where do ye think this one's leadin' ye now?"

Angus took a sip, eyes flicking between them. "That's the question, isn't it?"

Before anything else could be said, the door burst open, and Elspeth stormed in like the very wind itself.

Maree nearly spilt her drink. "What in blazes—?"

Elspeth's eyes were wild with delight. "Och, ye should see the moon tonight! It's dancin' like fire on the hills!"

Angus, eyebrows raised, turned to Dougal. "Who's this?"

Dougal sighed, rubbing his face. "Angus, meet Elspeth. Resident madwoman, spiritual guide, and occasional nuisance."

Elspeth scoffed. "Och, and ye're the expert, are ye?" She turned back to Angus, eyes gleaming. "Well, if ye've got any adventure left in yer bones, come see for yerself! The wind's still high, and the moon's burnin' bright enough to light up the whole moor!"

Angus chuckled, standing. "Why not? I've seen moons in jungles and moons in deserts. Might as well see how the Highlands compare."

Maree groaned. "Elspeth, if ye make me run through the moors, I swear—"

But the old woman grabbed her hand, tugging her toward the door. "Och, stop grumblin', lass! The night's young, and ye've got love in yer heart!"

Maree shot a glare at Dougal over her shoulder, but he just grinned, following them out.

The wind had settled into a steady breeze, and above them, the moon truly did shine like silver fire, illuminating the moors in ghostly light.

Elspeth twirled, arms raised, letting the wind pull at her skirts. Angus laughed, shaking his head.

Maree, despite herself, laughed too. She took Dougal's hand and squeezed it, letting the cool night air fill her lungs.

For the first time in a long while, everything felt exactly as it should be.

Angus stood at the edge of the ridge, watching the rolling hills beneath the moon. He was smiling, but there was something else there too—something unspoken, something unreadable.

He hadn't meant to linger. But now that he was here, something in the land stirred—a recognition, a question, perhaps even a reckoning. The moors didn't just welcome; they watched. They listened.

Because no matter what he had told them, Angus MacLeod had not come home only to see his cousin.

And as the wind whispered through the heather, carrying secrets too light for the human ear, it seemed to know it too.

CHAPTER 11

HARVEST FESTIVAL

As autumn painted the Highland landscape in warm hues, the community gathered in joyous anticipation for the annual Harvest Festival, a celebration that had echoed through generations. The air carried the crisp scent of fallen leaves and the promise of abundance, setting the stage for a revelry that united the Highland spirits.

Maree, Dougal, and Angus found themselves woven into the fabric of festival preparations. The croft, adorned with wildflowers and heather, became a hive of activity. Baskets overflowed with the season's bounty—plump apples, golden grains, and the last of the summer vegetables. The moors, which had provided sustenance throughout the year, now yielded their gifts in full, a testament to the rhythm of Highland life.

The trio worked side by side, their laughter mingling with the rustle of leaves as they decorated the festival grounds. Angus, his hands worn by both Highland winds and foreign landscapes, regaled them with tales of harvest celebrations from distant corners of the world. Maree, rooted in the traditions passed down through her family, wove the essence of the moors into every garland and wreath. And Dougal—once a man restless for horizons unknown—found himself at ease, working alongside them, no longer feeling the pull to leave.

As they strung heather across the festival entrance, Maree began humming a Celtic tune, her voice lifting into the crisp air. Dougal caught on, adding his own low harmony, and before long, their voices blended in a familiar song that had been sung over the moors for centuries.

Angus, watching them with a grin, tapped his fingers against an upturned barrel to keep time. "Ah, the music of the Highlands," he mused. "It can bring even the weariest traveller back to life. Reminds me of a ceilidh I once stumbled upon in the heart of Dublin—entire city seemed to move to the same tune."

Maree's eyes twinkled. "Well, we might not have Dublin's streets, but we have the moors. And that's a dance floor like no other."

He smiled at that, but his gaze lingered on the heather beyond the stone wall. There was a quietness in his eyes, just for a moment, like a shadow passing over the hills. A man could journey across continents and still find himself waiting for something only the wind could name.

The Harvest Festival, steeped in tradition, unfolded in a joyous celebration. Highland reels echoed through the glens as villagers, clad in tartan and woven headdresses, twirled beneath the open sky. Children darted between the dancers, their faces painted with the vibrant colours of autumn, their laughter ringing as they joined in the merriment.

Long tables groaned under the weight of a feast fit for the Highlands—stews rich with herbs from the moors, fresh-baked bannocks, and roasted meats slow-cooked to perfection. Wild berries from the hillsides sweetened the desserts, their tartness balanced by honey gathered from the heather-clad slopes. The aroma of spiced cider mixed with the smoky scent of the bonfire, creating a warmth that wrapped around the gathering like a well-loved plaid.

Elspeth, dressed in her finest shawl stitched with forget-me-nots and foxglove, moved through the crowd like a sprightly ghost of the glens—offering blessings, predictions, and the occasional cheeky pinch to startled bachelors. "The harvest is rich," she declared, eyes gleaming, "and so are the hearts gathered here tonight!"

Old Duncan, the village storyteller, held the crowd in rapt attention with tales of mythical creatures that roamed the moors. Beside him, Jenny, the healer, moved through the throng, offering sprigs of dried heather for luck. The festival was a living tapestry of Highland life, woven together by the shared laughter, the music, and the deep-rooted kinship of those who called this land home.

For Maree, Dougal, and Angus, the festival felt like more than a gathering—it was a reflection of how their lives had intertwined. As they stood together, watching the villagers dance and feast beneath the stars, the lines between Highlander and wanderer blurred.

They had all sought something different: Maree, a steadfast life on the land; Dougal, a place where his restless heart could settle; Angus, a home he wasn't sure he'd ever find. And yet, here they were—together, in the heart of the moors that had drawn them back like an old song too familiar to ignore.

Angus felt it stirring again, that odd sensation of being both grounded and adrift. The songs, the scent of peat smoke, the thrum of the earth underfoot—it all tugged at something old inside him. Something he hadn't dared to claim as belonging.

As the night wore on, the reels grew wilder, the fiddles and pipes lifting in joyful defiance of the encroaching cold. Maree found herself swept up in the dancing, her boots kicking up the earth as she was twirled in and out of the lively throng.

Angus, watching from the edge of the firelight, shook his head, laughing. "Maree, ye've got a step in yer boots that'd put any Spanish dancer to shame."

Maree, breathless but grinning, called back, "And what's stoppin' you from joinin' in, then?"

Angus lifted his whisky with a smirk. "This," he said, taking a slow sip.

Dougal, standing beside him, gave him a nudge. "Och, come now. The moors have missed yer footsteps, cousin. It's good to have ye back, wanderer or not."

Angus hesitated, then tipped his head. "Aye. It's good to be back."

They wandered toward the bonfire, settling onto one of the low stone walls as laughter and dancing carried on around them. The flames flickered in golden arcs, casting long shadows against the ancient stones of the village square.

With a mischievous glint in his eye, Angus launched into one of his many tales—this one about a particularly stubborn goat he'd once encountered in the markets of Marrakech, a creature determined to steal his entire satchel of dried figs.

Maree nearly spat out her cider laughing. "And what did ye do?"

"What could I do?" Angus shrugged. "I lost. The bloody goat won."

Dougal shook his head. "Och, ye've wrestled with the rivers of Patagonia, and yet a goat bested ye?"

Angus lifted his cup, undeterred. "Even a great man has his weaknesses."

Maree, still chuckling, raised her own cup. "To new beginnings, then. To laughter, and foolish goats, and the bonds of friendship."

Dougal and Angus lifted their cups in agreement. "Slàinte mhath!"

The cups clinked, the sound ringing through the Highland night, mingling with the music, the wind, and the soft rustling of the heather.

And so, beneath the open sky, with the moors watching in quiet approval, they celebrated—not just the harvest, but the roots they had begun to plant in one another's lives.

For some, it had taken years of wandering. For others, it had always been here, waiting.

But in the flickering firelight, there was no doubt—this was home.

SHADOWS OF THE PAST

As the echoes of the Harvest Festival lingered in the Highland air, a shadow emerged from Angus's past, threatening to cast a chill over the newfound harmony of the trio.

Whispers of Angus's mysterious history had long stirred intrigue through the moors, but now, those whispers took form—a figure from another life stepping onto Highland soil, carrying the weight of unresolved tales and unforeseen consequences.

Maree, always attuned to the subtle shifts of the land, felt the impending storm before she saw it. Dougal, watching Angus closely, sensed it too. His cousin, usually so at ease, had grown restless these past days, his gaze drifting toward the horizon as if expecting something—or someone.

And then, the past arrived.

The man who came seeking Angus bore the weight of shared history and unspoken truths, demanding resolution. The moors, once a sanctuary, now became the stage for a confrontation that transcended mere words.

The first time Maree saw Eoin Caird, she felt it in her gut—a heaviness that wrapped around the croft like a chill wind. He wasn't a stranger in the usual sense; he was something older, something unresolved. Even Elspeth, watching from the garden path, narrowed her eyes and muttered something about ghosts not staying buried long.

Maree and Dougal stood by Angus's side, solid and unyielding as the storm gathered. The croft, which had witnessed laughter and camaraderie, now became a refuge where they would face whatever ghosts Angus had left behind. The fire crackled low in the hearth, its flickering light mirroring the uncertainty on Angus's face.

The shadow from his past took form in Eoin Caird—an old comrade from his gold-mining days in South America. They had once worked side by side, panning rivers in the Amazon, navigating the treacherous foothills of the Andes, and living off their wits and the land in search of fortune. But fortune had not come without cost.

Eoin had tracked him down, not for a reunion, but for answers.

"Angus," Eoin said, standing at the croft's threshold, his eyes hard with accusation, "it's been years. I've travelled a long way to find you."

Angus met his gaze with a measured calm, but something in his posture tensed. "Eoin," he said, his voice quieter than usual. "I never thought I'd see ye again."

Maree and Dougal exchanged a glance, sensing the weight in those words.

Eoin stepped forward, his boots heavy on the wooden floor. "We were comrades once," he continued, "and then... nothing. No word. No trace. I need to understand why."

Angus exhaled slowly, raking a hand through his hair. "What happened in those jungles... I didn't expect ye to come all this way."

Eoin's jaw tightened. "We were driven out, Angus. Marked as outcasts. The villagers turned their backs on us. And I was left to defend our actions alone. You disappeared when I needed you most."

Silence settled over the croft, thick and unmoving.

Dougal, always quick to defend kin, folded his arms. "And what exactly happened between ye?"

Eoin didn't take his eyes off Angus. "Tell them," he said, voice low. "Tell them about the gold we found, the people we crossed, and the price we paid."

Maree frowned, glancing between them. "Angus?"

Angus's hands curled into fists, though his voice remained level. "The Amazon is no place for the greedy. We found something we weren't meant to. Gold, yes—but sacred gold. It belonged to the land, to the people who lived there long before us. I knew it. Ye knew it, too, Eoin."

Eoin let out a sharp breath. "Aye, I did. But ye left me behind to bear the brunt of it!" His frustration cracked through the room like thunder. "The villagers cursed us, called us thieves, and I had to face them alone while ye vanished into the jungle like a ghost."

Angus closed his eyes briefly, the memory pressing down on him. "I didn't vanish. I stayed behind. I tried to make it right, but the damage was already done." His voice was heavy with regret. "Ye think I walked away easy, Eoin? I lost everything, same as you."

Eoin's fists clenched at his sides. "Ye could have written, could have sent word that ye were alive. Do ye know what it was like, defendin' our names while the man I thought was my closest friend was nowhere to be found?"

Angus exhaled, his voice quiet but firm. "I wasn't lookin' for forgiveness when I left South America. And I'm not lookin' for it now."

There was a flicker of something old in Angus's expression—shame, yes, but also the grief of a man who had carried a burden alone for too long. Maree stepped closer, placing a hand gently on his arm. She didn't speak—didn't need to. Her presence grounded him.

"Then what are ye lookin' for, Angus?" Eoin demanded. "Because I want answers. I want to know if ye regret it, if ye even care what happened."

Angus, his eyes shadowed with old grief, held Eoin's gaze. "I care," he said simply. "I always did."

For a moment, the weight of the past pressed down upon them. The Highland mist swirled outside, caught in the wind, mirroring the unresolved tension between the two men. The firelight flickered, throwing long shadows across the croft walls, as the truth of old betrayals and unfinished business settled between them like an untamed beast.

Outside, the wind picked up again, as if the land itself sensed the shift. The trees bowed slightly, and a raven took flight from the fencepost, circling once before vanishing into the grey.

Then, after what felt like an eternity, Eoin stepped back, his expression unreadable.

"Fine," he said at last. "Then let's settle this properly. No more shadows. No more runnin'."

Angus nodded, a slow, measured motion. "Aye. No more runnin'."

The moors, silent and watchful, bore witness to a reckoning long overdue.

Maree and Dougal, standing as quiet sentinels, exchanged a glance. Whatever was coming next, they would face it together.

The past had come knocking—but the present, and the bonds they had forged here, would decide what happened next.

CHAPTER 13

UNVEILING OF DOUGAL

The evening settled softly around the croft.

Outside, the moors stretched beneath a sky painted with fading gold and deepening violet. The last rays of sunlight lingered upon the distant hills before surrendering to dusk.

Inside, the fire burned warmly.

Maree sat near the hearth mending a tear in one of Dougal's shirts, while Angus occupied his usual chair, a mug balanced precariously on one knee.

For a time, nobody spoke.

The silence was comfortable.

The sort that comes from friendship rather than emptiness.

Yet Dougal found himself staring into the flames.

Lost in thought.

Eventually Angus noticed.

"Ye've got that look again."

Dougal glanced up.

"What look?"

"The one that says yer somewhere else entirely."

Maree smiled faintly without looking up from her stitching.

"Aye. He's been wearin' it all evening."

Dougal sighed.

"Have I?"

"Aye."

Angus leaned forward.

"Out with it."

The fire crackled softly.

Dougal hesitated.

He wasn't accustomed to speaking about such things.

Truthfully, he wasn't entirely sure why the subject had returned to him now.

Perhaps it was because, for the first time in years, he felt settled.

Or perhaps because some questions grew louder the longer they were ignored.

"There was a place me father used tae mention."

Maree looked up.

"A place?"

"Aye."

Dougal rubbed the back of his neck.

"He only ever spoke of it a handful o' times."

Angus raised an eyebrow.

"That alone makes it worth hearing."

A smile tugged briefly at Dougal's mouth.

His father had not been a man given to stories.

Most conversations had been practical.

Brief.

Final.

Yet every now and then, usually late at night when whisky loosened old memories, a different man emerged.

A quieter man.

A sadder one.

"There was a name."

The room seemed to grow still.

"Clachanoch."

Neither Maree nor Angus spoke.

The name itself felt old.

Older than any of them.

Dougal stared into the fire.

"I was just a lad when I first heard it."

"What is it?" Maree asked.

He shook his head.

"That's the trouble."

"You dinnae know?"

"Nae."

Angus laughed.

"So this grand mystery begins with ye knowin' absolutely nothin'."

"More or less."

The laughter eased the tension.

Yet the name remained.

Lingering.

Like smoke.

Dougal leaned back in his chair.

"Me father never explained much. If I asked questions, he'd shut down faster than a winter door."

"Sounds familiar," Angus muttered.

Maree smirked.

Dougal ignored them both.

"The little I gathered was that Clachanoch was once connected tae our family."

"Connected how?" Maree asked.

Again, he shrugged.

"I only know fragments."

The admission frustrated him.

He preferred certainty.

Facts.

Solid ground beneath his feet.

Yet Clachanoch refused to provide any.

There were only pieces.

A faded journal.

A few sketches.

A handful of stories.

Nothing complete.

Nothing clear.

"I remember finding an old drawing once."

Maree set aside her sewing.

"What sort of drawing?"

"A house."

His voice softened.

"A grand one."

For a moment the image returned with startling clarity.

Tall windows.

Stone walls.

Sweeping grounds.

A place built to endure.

Yet even in the sketch there had been a strange sadness.

As though something important had already been lost.

"It looked abandoned."

The fire shifted.

Shadows danced across the walls.

"Did yer father live there?" Angus asked.

"Nae."

"His father?"

"Nae."

"Then who?"

Dougal laughed quietly.

"If I knew that, we wouldnae be havin' this conversation."

The three of them smiled.

Yet curiosity had taken root.

Maree could feel it.

So could Angus.

And if he was honest, so could Dougal.

For years he had dismissed the stories.

Told himself they didn't matter.

Yet lately the name had returned with increasing frequency.

Clachanoch.

A whisper in the back of his thoughts.

A half-remembered melody.

A question waiting for an answer.

"There was one thing me father said."

The room quietened once more.

Dougal rarely spoke about his father.

When he did, people listened.

"He said some places remember."

A strange chill passed through him.

The exact same words had haunted him for years.

Maree exchanged a glance with Angus.

Neither spoke.

Outside, the wind moved softly across the moors.

Almost as though the Highlands themselves were listening.

"What did he mean?" Maree finally asked.

Dougal stared into the flames.

"Nae idea."

And that was the truth.

The old man had never explained.

Perhaps he couldn't.

Perhaps he wouldn't.

Or perhaps some memories hurt too much to share.

The fire burned lower.

The croft settled around them.

Old timbers creaked softly overhead.

After a while Angus stood and stretched.

"Well."

He drained the last of his tea.

"That's the most mysterious conversation I've had all week."

Dougal chuckled.

"Sorry tae disappoint ye."

"Nae."

Angus moved toward the door.

"I've a feelin' this story's only just beginning."

The words hung in the air after he left.

Only Maree and Dougal remained.

The firelight flickered between them.

"Do ye think it's important?" she asked quietly.

Dougal considered the question.

For years he would have answered no.

Without hesitation.

Yet now?

Now he wasn't so sure.

He looked toward the window.

Beyond the glass, darkness had settled across the moors.

Ancient.

Patient.

Waiting.

"Aye," he said softly.

"I think it might be."

Maree reached across and squeezed his hand.

No more questions followed.

None were needed.

Because for the first time in his life, Dougal McBeth had stopped running long enough to wonder where he came from.

And somewhere beyond the hills, beyond memory, beyond the reach of forgotten generations, the first threads of an old story were beginning to stir.

EOIN'S DEMANDS

In the annals of Angus MacLeod and Eoin Caird's shared history, there existed a chapter forged in the gold-laden rivers of South America, where the echoes of their wanderlust and adventurous spirits intertwined. More than comrades, they were brothers of the road, traversing continents and delving into the mysteries of foreign lands, bound by a camaraderie as unyielding as the Highland rock.

Their paths first diverged in the Amazon basin, where they had spent years panning for gold, following the lure of fortune that had drawn countless men into the depths of the jungle. They had seen rivers run rich with gold dust, had worked shoulder to shoulder with native tribes who knew the land's secrets, had celebrated under the jungle moonlight when they struck lucky, and fought bitterly when the rush turned to desperation.

But it wasn't greed that had shattered them. It was something far more human.

In a remote village, nestled deep within the rainforest, Angus and Eoin had stumbled into a conflict not of their making—one that would change everything.

A division had formed among the villagers, between those who wished to preserve their sacred land and those tempted by the riches buried beneath it. The discovery of gold veins running beneath the village soil had stirred dreams of wealth, but also fear of destruction.

Eoin and Angus, drawn into the fray, found themselves fighting not for riches, but for justice. The tribal elders feared the land's desecration; the younger men saw an escape from poverty. The village was torn in two, and despite their best efforts, Angus and Eoin only made things worse.

They chose a side—they stood with the elders, defending the sacred lands, speaking against the foreign prospectors who sought to strip the land bare. But their intervention came at a cost.

The violence escalated.

The village fell into chaos.

What had been a place of peace turned into a battlefield.

When the gold hunters retaliated, it was the elders who suffered first. The sacred site was burned, and those who had fought to protect it were exiled. The younger men, emboldened, took the land for themselves, and turned against the very men who had tried to help them.

Eoin and Angus were driven out. Accused of betrayal, they became pariahs, left to watch as the village destroyed itself in the wake of their choices.

They had set out to protect—but in the end, they had only brought ruin.

The scars of that failure ran deeper than any knife wound.

The jungle had swallowed their innocence. Even now, years later, Angus could still hear the chants of the villagers echoing through the trees, could still see the sacred stones being toppled and burned. It haunted his sleep, lingered in the creases of his palms like the soil had embedded itself into his bones.

Angus, embittered and furious, had blamed Eion for persuading him to take a stand. He had wanted to leave, to let the village decide its own fate—but Eion, always the idealist, had insisted they fight. And so, when they were cast out, Angus turned his back on Eion and left him to wander alone.

They had not spoken since.

Now, in the Highland mist, beneath the stars so far removed from the jungle sky, Angus faced the man who had once been his closest brother, and the demands of the past could no longer be ignored.

Eoin's arrival in the Highlands was not by chance.

He had come seeking resolution. But not peace.

"You disappeared, Angus." His voice was a blade, sharp and unyielding. "When the village burned, when the elders were cast out, when I stood alone, you vanished. I needed you, and you were gone."

Angus met his gaze, something old and unspoken passing between them. "Ye think I abandoned ye?" His voice, though calm, was laced with sorrow. "Eoin, I was lost. I was ashamed. We tried to do right, and instead, we tore those people apart."

Eoin's jaw clenched. "They trusted us."

"Aye." Angus nodded slowly. "And we failed them."

The words hung in the air, heavy as the Highland mist.

Then, after a long pause, Eoin exhaled sharply. "Do ye ever think about going back?"

Angus blinked. "Back?"

"To the Amazon."

The very idea set Angus's heart pounding.

He looked around the croft, the thick stone walls sheltering him, the scent of peat smoke clinging to his skin. The jungle felt like a dream now, distant, fevered, impossible. Yet something stirred beneath his ribs, something unfinished.

Eoin's eyes blazed. "We left a mess, Angus. Maybe it's time we faced it. Maybe it's time we made it right."

Angus rubbed a hand over his jaw, staring into the fire. The Highland winds whispered, as if stirring the ghosts of their past.

Could they?

Would it even matter?

Would the people even want them back?

And yet, the thought took root.

In the shadows of the croft, Elspeth watched the two men silently.

And then, she smiled.

"Ach, ye fools," she said, shaking her head. "Always runnin', always searchin'. D'ye no' see?"

Angus and Eoin turned to her.

She stepped closer, the firelight catching the silver in her hair. "There's a reason yer paths crossed again. The moors have a way o' callin' folk home—but they also send 'em where they're needed. If yer hearts tell ye there's unfinished business in the Amazon, then maybe ye've still got work to do."

A gust of wind rattled the shutters. In its wake came a stillness so complete that even the fire seemed to pause. The croft felt like a pause in time, suspended between past and present, waiting.

Angus, eyes shadowed, looked back at Eoin. "And what if it's too late?"

Elspeth shrugged. "Aye, well. That's for the jungle to decide."

She turned on her heel and, with a laugh, disappeared into the night—a ghost on the wind, a whisper of Highland magic.

Angus watched her go, then glanced back at Eoin.

The road was calling again.

And this time, he might not walk it alone.

HIGHLAND PROPOSAL

The Highland sky stretched vast and endless above them, stars emerging one by one as twilight settled across the moors. The scent of heather drifted upon the wind, mingling with the damp earth and distant peat smoke.

Dougal McBeth drew a slow breath.

For all his wanderings, he had never felt so certain of anything.

He had crossed deserts beneath foreign suns, watched the northern lights dance across frozen skies, and walked among ruins older than memory. Yet none of those places had ever felt like home.

Home stood beside him now.

Maree Doonagan.

The wind tugged playfully at her auburn hair as she stared out across the hills, entirely unaware of the battle taking place inside his chest.

He had faced storms with less fear than this.

Hidden safely in his pocket rested the ring he had purchased in town. It wasn't extravagant. Maree would have hated extravagant. The simple band had been fashioned from Highland gold and engraved with a tiny thistle—a symbol of strength, endurance, and stubborn survival.

In other words, Maree herself.

"Why have ye dragged me all the way up here?" she asked, narrowing her eyes suspiciously. "I've still work waiting back at the croft."

Dougal smiled despite himself.

Some things never changed.

"Aye, I ken."

"Then this had better be important."

"It is."

Something in his voice must have reached her.

Maree's teasing expression softened.

The wind moved through the heather around them. Somewhere below, a deer stepped quietly through the bracken.

For a brief moment, the Highlands seemed to pause.

Dougal reached into his pocket.

Then, before he could lose his nerve, he dropped to one knee.

Maree froze.

Her eyes widened.

For once, she appeared completely speechless.

It was a rare and remarkable sight.

"Dinnae look so shocked," Dougal muttered.

That earned a startled laugh.

Then he held out the ring.

"Maree Doonagan."

His voice steadied.

"I've spent half my life running."

The smile faded from her face.

"But every road I've walked has somehow led me back tae ye."

The wind stirred softly around them.

"I canna promise riches."

Maree snorted.

"I'd be worried if ye did."

"Aye, fair enough."

He smiled briefly before continuing.

"I canna promise there'll never be hardships."

"Definitely worried now."

That earned another laugh from both of them.

But then his expression grew serious.

"What I can promise is this."

He held her gaze.

"No more running."

The words settled between them.

Simple.

Honest.

True.

"I choose ye, Maree. Today. Tomorrow. And every day after that."

Emotion flickered across her face.

Love.

Relief.

Disbelief.

Hope.

"Maree Doonagan... will ye marry me?"

For a heartbeat she simply stared.

Then tears appeared in her eyes.

Not many.

Just enough.

"Aye, ye daft fool."

Her voice trembled.

"Aye."

Dougal barely had time to stand before she threw herself into his arms.

The ring nearly disappeared into the heather.

Neither noticed.

Far across the hillside, hidden behind a boulder, Elspeth shook her head.

"Took them long enough."

The news travelled through the glen with astonishing speed.

By the following evening, the croft had transformed into a celebration.

Wildflowers decorated the tables.

Lanterns hung from beams overhead.

The smell of baking, roasting meat, and fresh bannocks filled every corner of the house.

Neighbours arrived carrying gifts.

Friends arrived carrying stories.

Relatives arrived carrying opinions.

The latter proved far more dangerous.

"About time," Fergus declared.

"It was only a matter of time," Isla agreed.

"Everybody knew it."

"Everybody except them," Caitriona added.

Maree buried her face in her hands.

Dougal found himself laughing.

Ewan merely stood nearby with folded arms and an expression that suggested he had expected this outcome for years.

Though Maree noticed the faint smile he kept trying to hide.

The evening unfolded in a blur of music, laughter, and celebration.

Fiddles played.

Children darted between tables.

Neighbours filled the croft with noise and warmth.

For a little while, every burden seemed lighter.

Even Angus allowed himself to enjoy the festivities.

That alone was worth celebrating.

Later, Elspeth rose with a dram in hand.

The room gradually quieted.

"To Dougal and Maree."

Her voice carried easily through the croft.

"May yer love endure like the hills around us."

She glanced knowingly at both of them.

"Stubborn. Unmovable. And occasionally difficult."

Laughter erupted around the room.

Elspeth lifted her glass.

"May ye face life's storms together, and may ye always remember that home is not a place."

Her gaze softened.

"It's the people who stand beside ye."

A chorus of agreement followed.

"Slàinte mhath!"

The room echoed the toast.

Glasses clinked.

Music resumed.

And the celebration carried on long into the night.

Much later, when most of the guests had drifted home and the music had softened to a gentle hum, Dougal and Maree slipped outside.

The stars blazed overhead.

The Highlands stretched endlessly before them.

Neither spoke.

Words weren't necessary.

Maree rested her head against his shoulder.

Dougal wrapped an arm around her.

The future remained uncertain.

Mysteries still waited beyond the horizon.

Journeys yet remained to be taken.

But for now, standing beneath the vast Highland sky, surrounded by family, friendship, and the land they loved, they allowed themselves a rare moment of peace.

Inside the croft, laughter still drifted through the open door.

Outside, the moors listened quietly.

And somewhere beyond the hills, other stories were already beginning.

NAVIGATING LOVE'S TERRAIN

The changing of the seasons had always brought a shift to the land, but this time, it carried a deeper transformation. Maree and Dougal's engagement was no longer just a promise spoken beneath the Highland stars—it was something tangible, as real as the soil beneath their feet. Their lives, once moving in separate currents, had now merged like two rivers meeting, steady and inevitable.

Preparations for the wedding had begun in earnest, not just in tasks and logistics, but in the quiet moments where their love settled into something deeper. Dougal no longer thought of the croft as Maree's; he saw it as their home. The work he put into the land was no longer about proving himself—it was the laying of foundations for the life they would build together.

Elspeth, ever watchful, saw the shift before either of them had even spoken of it. She was a woman who had spent her life reading signs—not just in the movement of the clouds or the rustling of the trees, but in the hearts of those around her. Now, as Maree and Dougal's bond strengthened, she knew the moors had more to say.

Angus, once a man accustomed to solitude, found himself settling into the communal life of the croft. The quiet warmth of companionship, the easy laughter shared over meals, and the simple joy of a shared purpose began to melt the walls he had built around himself.

In the evenings, Angus often found himself lingering near the hearth after supper, content just to listen. The clink of mugs, the murmur of familiar voices, and the occasional bark of laughter had become as vital to him as the breath in his lungs. It was unfamiliar—and yet, strangely comforting.

Then, as if guided by the unseen forces that wove through the Highlands, a new presence arrived—Fiona Cameron.

A woman of means and experience, Fiona had seen the world beyond the Highlands. Her confidence was matched only by her kindness, and though her years had gifted her with streaks of silver through her dark brown hair, they had also imparted a wisdom that made her presence one of quiet reassurance. She carried herself with the air of someone who had lived fully—her adventures spanning bustling cities and remote corners of the earth—but despite all she had seen, it was the Highlands that called her home.

Her arrival was not abrupt; rather, it felt as though she had always belonged here, stepping seamlessly into the croft's ever-evolving story. She had been travelling through nearby villages when she heard of Dougal's return, and curiosity had drawn her to the croft—though, as she later admitted with a knowing smile, perhaps something deeper had guided her steps.

Elspeth would later say she felt it the moment Fiona's boots first touched Highland soil again—the way the moors responded, the hush that fell, as though recognising a soul who had wandered far only to return home.

One afternoon, as Angus worked by the croft, mending a fence that had taken the brunt of the last storm, he sensed movement in the distance. Looking up, he saw Fiona approaching, her steps measured yet unhurried, as if she belonged to the land as much as the wind that carried her forward.

"Guid day tae ye, Fiona," Angus greeted, tipping his hat slightly, the sound of his own brogue catching him off guard. It had been so long since he had spoken with someone who made him feel so rooted in his homeland.

Fiona's eyes twinkled. "Aye, Angus, it's a braw day indeed. The moors seem to be whisperin' of adventures today."

Amused, Angus arched a brow. "Aye, they do that. Ye've a keen ear for the moors' secrets, it seems."

Fiona chuckled, tilting her head as if listening. "Aye, a lifetime o' listenin' will do that to ye. The land speaks, if ye care to hear it."

Angus studied her for a moment, his curiosity deepening. "Ye've a way wi' words, Fiona. That's a rare thing."

She gestured toward the croft, her smile warm. "Let me no' keep ye from yer work. I'm here tae help, if there's aught I can do."

A slow smile tugged at Angus's lips. "Aye, we're a wee family here at the croft, and an extra hand is always welcome."

"Then consider me a friend and a helpin' hand," she said simply. "Let's make the most o' this fine day."

And so, they worked together, their movements unhurried, their conversation meandering between the present and the past, the Highlands and distant lands. The moors, ever observant, seemed to hum in quiet approval.

By the time the sun dipped low, casting the hills in honeyed gold, Angus realised he hadn't once felt the weight that usually settled on his shoulders by day's end. In its place was something new. Not quite hope—but the promise of it.

As the days passed, Fiona's presence became as natural as the morning mist that rolled over the hills. She was no outsider, nor was she merely a visitor—she was a woman with her own history, her own burdens, yet she carried them with grace. And Angus, who had long guarded his heart, found himself drawn to her quiet strength.

For Maree and Dougal, love had been a storm—wild, untamed, fierce in its arrival. For Angus and Fiona, it was something altogether different. It was steady as the Highland rivers carving their way through stone, shaping the land over time, quiet but undeniable.

Elspeth, ever attuned to the moors and their secrets, found herself drawn to Fiona. There was something about her, something ancient yet familiar, as though the land itself had called her home.

One mist-laden morning, Elspeth found Fiona standing at the edge of the moors, gazing toward the hills as if listening to a voice just beyond reach.

"Ye hear them, don't ye?" Elspeth murmured, stepping beside her.

Fiona turned, a knowing look in her eyes. "Aye. The moors have been whisperin' to me since I set foot here."

Elspeth nodded, satisfied. "Then ye ken that their whispers are never idle. They speak of change... of things still to come."

Fiona studied her for a long moment. "And what is it they tell ye, Elspeth?"

The older woman turned her gaze to the horizon, her voice low and certain. "A union is comin', one that's been long in the makin'. Maree and Dougal, they're tethered now, their lives bound by the land itself. But there's more." She turned back to Fiona, her eyes sharp. "The moors speak of shadows yet to be cast. There's work to be done, wounds to mend, reckonings to be faced."

Fiona exhaled slowly, the truth settling into her bones. "Aye, I feel it too," she admitted. "And not just for them. The past is no' finished wi' Angus yet."

Elspeth's lips curled into a wry smile. "Och, that lad. He thinks he can outrun fate, but the moors always bring folk back to where they're meant to be."

Fiona chuckled softly, though her gaze remained thoughtful. "And what o' me, Elspeth? What do the moors whisper about my place in all this?"

The older of the women tilted her head, listening to something distant. Then, with a nod, she said, "Ye were meant to come here, Fiona Cameron. The land knew it long afore ye did. Ye'll stand where ye're needed most."

Neither woman spoke again for some time. They simply stood there—two silhouettes at the edge of the moor, listening to the secrets only the wind could carry. The silence between them held more than words ever could.

The weight of those words lingered between them, unspoken yet undeniable.

Meanwhile, at the croft, life continued in its steady rhythm. Maree and Dougal worked side by side, their hands dirty from the soil, their laughter carried on the breeze. Angus, once a man destined to walk alone, found himself drawn to Fiona's presence, their companionship unfolding in quiet understanding.

It was a time of both grounding and anticipation. The wedding would come soon, but the moors whispered that there was still more to unfold. And those who listened—Maree, Dougal, Angus, Elspeth, and now Fiona—knew better than to ignore the call of the land.

HIGHLAND VOWS

As midsummer embraced the Highland moors, the croft bustled with preparations for a celebration that would weave itself into the very tapestry of the land. The winds carried the scent of heather, the earth hummed with the pulse of tradition, and beneath the vast sky, a makeshift archway stood—its frame entwined with wildflowers, its roots sunk deep into the soil, as though the moors themselves had conspired to witness this moment.

Maree stood beneath that archway, her cream-coloured gown flowing like the waters of a Highland loch. Delicate ribbons fluttered in the breeze, woven into her long hair alongside sprigs of purple heather. The anticipation in her heart was matched only by the soft glow in her eyes as she gazed at Dougal. He stood tall beside her, dressed in

Highland finery, the McBeth tartan draped proudly over his shoulder—a pattern stitched with history, whispering of kin and kings who had walked these lands before him.

Above them, the sun broke through a thin veil of cloud, casting golden light over the gathered guests. The warmth kissed Maree's shoulders and caught in the weave of Dougal's tartan, as if the heavens themselves had come to bless the day. Children giggled in the distance, wildflowers tucked behind their ears, and even the sheep on the hillside seemed to bleat in approval.

The vows they spoke were not just words; they were echoes carried by the mist, binding them not only to each other but to the moors, to the past and future alike.

"By the ancient stones and the whisperin' winds, I pledge my heart to you, Maree," Dougal vowed, his voice steady as the hills that bore witness.

Maree, her voice just as resolute, responded, "In the light of the Highland stars and the embrace of the heathers, I give ye my heart, Dougal, for now and always."

As their hands met, a hush fell over the moors. Then, with the tenderness of a promise fulfilled, Dougal cupped her cheek and pressed a kiss to her lips, sealing their vows beneath the wide Highland sky. The gathered heathers seemed to bow in reverence, and when the moment passed, a joyous cheer erupted from the crowd.

Among the guests, tears glistened in more than one eye. Even Angus, usually a man of stoic expression, found himself blinking against the emotion welling up. Elspeth squeezed his hand, her old fingers warm and steady, and whispered, "A rare thing, this kind o' love. We don't just witness it—we carry it with us."

The croft, once a quiet homestead, now pulsed with revelry. Laughter rang out, hands clapped in time to the music, and voices lifted in song.

Isla Doonagan, with her fiddle, struck up a lively tune, and soon the croft became a dance floor beneath the Highland sun. Neighbours joined hands in a spirited reel, skirts twirling, kilts swinging, feet pounding the earth in celebration. The air was thick with the scent of roasted meats and fresh bannocks, with the warmth of whisky shared among friends.

Amidst it all, Angus found himself drawn into the fold. Solitude had been his constant companion for years, but here, now, he felt something stir within him—something warm, something like home. Fiona, by his side, met his gaze with a knowing smile, and together they became part of the fabric of the night, another thread woven into the tapestry of the moors.

Near the bonfire, children skipped and sang old Highland songs, their voices rising above the crackle of flames. Elders swapped stories passed down through generations, their weathered faces lit with mirth and memory. This was more than a wedding—it was a gathering of lifeblood, a celebration not just of two souls, but of a people rooted in land and legacy.

At the heart of the festivities stood the Doonagan siblings—Ewan, Isla, Fergus, and Caitriona—leading the ceilidh with music and laughter, their voices rising in harmony with the wind. When the dancing slowed, Ewan's wife, Morag, stepped forward, parchment in hand, and silence fell as she recited words steeped in Highland tradition:

In the heart of the Highlands, where heather blooms,
Two souls entwined, where love resumes.
Dougal, with eyes like the Highland morn,
Maree, in whom grace and strength are born.
Beneath the skies, so vast and grand,
Their love like rivers, eternally planned.
Maree, a rose in the Highland glade,
Dougal, the oak in love's sweet shade.
Through moorland mist, their journey unfolds,
A tale of passion, as ancient as the wolds.
Maree's laughter, a Highland stream's sweet song,
Dougal's gaze, steady, where they belong.
As heather blushes 'neath the setting sun,
Their love, like rivers, forever to run.
Dougal, a bard with tales untold,
Maree, a tale of silver and gold.
So, let the winds whisper through the glen,
Of love that's true, now and again.
In this Highland land, where dreams take flight,
Dougal and Maree, love's pure light.

As Morag finished, the poem hung in the air, settling like mist over the crowd. Then, Angus stepped forward, holding a Quaich filled with the finest Highland whisky. The firelight danced against the silver vessel as he spoke, his voice carrying the weight of tradition.

"May this Quaich, a vessel of shared trust and unity, symbolise the bond ye forge today. As ye drink from its cup, may it mark the beginnin' of a journey filled wi' strength, laughter, and endurin' love."

Maree and Dougal, hands joined, each took hold of a handle of the Quaich, sharing a sip from its ancient vessel. The warmth of the whisky, the meaning behind it, settled deep within them, binding their love not just in the eyes of their people but in the very spirit of the Highlands.

As twilight fell, lanterns were lit around the croft, their soft glow dancing like will-o'-the-wisps across the fields. The sound of music continued, but it grew gentler, more intimate, echoing the shift from celebration to reflection. Beneath the stars, couples swayed, children dozed in laps, and a gentle hush settled over the moor.

Elspeth rose then, her presence commanding and serene. As the firelight cast long shadows, she raised her hands, blessing them with a Gaelic benediction:

Go raibh tú daibhir i mí-áidh
  Agus saibhir i mbeannachtaí
  Go mall ag déanamh namhaid, go luath a déanamh carad,
  Agus go mbuailimid le chéile arís,
  Go gcoinní Dia i mbos A láimhe thú.
  (May you be poor in misfortune,
  Rich in blessings,
  Slow to make enemies, quick to make friends,

And may you know nothing but happiness from this day forward.)

As her words settled over them, the crowd erupted once more, lifting their voices in song, their feet returning to the dance.

Under the Highland stars, amidst the embrace of the moors, Maree and Dougal's love story reached its crescendo—not an ending, but a beginning. The archway adorned in heather stood tall behind them, a silent witness to this sacred union. The night stretched long, filled with laughter, music, and the promise of all that was to come.

* * *

Later, long after the last song had faded and only embers glowed in the fire pit, Dougal and Maree stood alone beneath the archway. He wrapped his arms around her, and they swayed gently in the quiet. "We're home," Maree whispered. Dougal nodded. "Aye, we are. And it's just the beginning."

As the celebration concluded, the moors whispered their approval, their voices carried on the wind, telling of love found, vows spoken, and a future waiting to unfold.

THE FOREBODING

After Maree and Dougal returned from their honeymoon in a nearby village, the croft was filled with a sense of newfound intimacy. Their bond, once built on fire and storm, had settled into something deeper—a tether to the land and to each other. Yet, as they stepped through the familiar doorway of their home, Elspeth stood waiting, her gaze heavy with unspoken words.

"There's somethin' brewin'," she said sternly, her voice carrying the weight of the moors themselves. "I dinnae ken what yet, but it's comin' tae these parts."

It was unlike Elspeth to prophesy doom and gloom. She spoke when she felt the land shift, when the moors whispered secrets only she seemed to hear. Maree, ever attuned to the croft and the rhythm of the Highlands, listened with rapt attention. Dougal, ever the rational one, couldn't shake the unease that settled in his bones after Elspeth's words.

That evening, as the sun dipped behind the hills, casting long shadows across the heather-covered land, Dougal, Maree, Angus, and Fiona gathered by the croft's hearth. The warm glow of the fire flickered against their faces, yet the air around them was heavy with tension.

"I dinnae usually pay heed tae prophecies or the like," Dougal admitted, rubbing a hand over his beard. "But there's a feelin' in the air... a restlessness I cannae shake."

Maree nodded, her hands wrapped around a warm cup. "Elspeth's warnings are rare, Dougal. When she speaks, it's 'cause the land has spoken first. We'd be fools tae ignore her."

Angus, his arms crossed, added gravely, "Aye, I've felt it too. The moors... they're breathin' different. Somethin's stirrin' beneath them."

Fiona, seated across from them, glanced toward the window where the wind had begun to pick up. "Even the animals ken it. The birds are restless, the sheep are jittery. It's as if the whole world is bracin' for somethin'."

* * *

That night, the dreams came. Each of them, sleeping restlessly, was visited by visions they couldn't quite explain. Maree dreamed of a figure cloaked in mist, standing at the edge of the moors. Dougal saw fire licking the sky above Clachanoch's ruins. Angus awoke with the scent of ash in his nose, and Fiona heard a voice calling her name in a language older than Gaelic. When morning broke, they said nothing, but the unease lingered.

Outside, the wind howled through the heather, rattling the croft's shutters. Maree stood and moved to the window, peering out at the darkened sky. The clouds swirled in an ominous dance, thick and brooding, a storm unlike any she had ever seen.

By the next morning, word had spread. The locals who lived in the valley and the neighbouring villages had heard the same reports—an unprecedented storm was on its way, a force of nature that would test the very foundations of the Highlands.

The air grew thick with tension as the storm gathered its strength. The once serene landscape of the moors transformed into a battlefield of wind and rain. The mist, once a gentle embrace over the hills, now clawed its way through the land, churning like an unsettled sea. Thunder rolled in the distance, a deep growl of warning.

The villagers worked frantically, securing roofs, lashing down livestock pens, reinforcing the old stone walls of their homes. Maree, Dougal, Angus, and Fiona laboured alongside them, their hands raw from rope and timber, their backs aching with the weight of preparation.

Elspeth, meanwhile, disappeared into the hills. She said little before leaving—only that she needed to speak with the stones, to listen to the winds in a place no others dared tread. Maree watched her go with a twist in her gut, sensing that the old woman carried more than just warnings. She carried a burden no one else yet understood.

As night fell, the storm descended.

The wind shrieked through the village, howling like a banshee, shaking even the sturdiest of stone-built crofts. Rain pounded the earth in torrents, drenching everything in its path. Trees bent and groaned beneath the force of the gales, their roots clinging desperately to the soil. The sky, black as pitch, split open with jagged forks of lightning that illuminated the chaos in ghostly flashes.

Inside the croft, the fire struggled against the drafts that pushed through the walls. Maree and Dougal sat close together, their hands clasped tightly, listening to the storm rage outside. Across the room, Angus paced, his expression grim.

"This isnae just a storm," he muttered. "It's somethin' else. It's as if the land itself is cryin' out."

Fiona, her face pale, nodded. "Aye... and it's demandin' we listen."

At the height of the gale, a strange pulse trembled beneath the ground. Maree felt it through the soles of her boots, like the heartbeat of something ancient waking. Dougal looked up sharply—he'd felt it too. Angus froze mid-step, his expression darkening, while Fiona whispered a prayer in a language none of them recognised.

The hours dragged on. The wind battered against the croft with such force that the walls trembled. They could hear the distant shattering of glass, the heavy thud of trees falling, the cries of frightened animals. At one point, the roof of the barn was torn away, carried off into the night like a leaf caught in a gale.

At the height of the storm, a terrible wailing rose above the roar of the wind—a deep, guttural sound that sent a chill down Maree's spine. It wasn't the cry of an animal. It was something older, something that belonged to the moors before men ever walked them.

Dougal's hand tightened around hers. "Ye heard that?"

Maree swallowed hard. "Aye. And I wish I hadnae."

The storm raged on for what felt like an eternity. But then, just before dawn, it ceased.

The stillness that followed was eerie, almost unnatural. The Highlands, usually so full of life, felt hollow, as if the storm had stolen something vital from them.

Maree and Dougal stepped outside and were met with devastation.

The village lay in ruin. Trees that had stood for generations were uprooted, their branches broken and twisted like shattered limbs. The once lush moors were reduced to a muddy wasteland, scattered with debris. The crofts, though sturdy, had not escaped unscathed—roofs were torn, walls crumbled, windows blown clean out of their frames. The livestock pens were decimated, and the mournful cries of wounded animals echoed through the wreckage.

Here and there, villagers stumbled out of their homes, faces pale with shock. Children clung to parents, elders wept openly, and farmers dropped to their knees amid ruined fields. Despite their own shock, Maree and Dougal moved from family to family, offering hands and shoulders, organising what little could be salvaged in the pale morning light.

The market square, usually bustling with life, was barely recognisable. Stalls lay in splinters, and personal belongings, flung by the winds, were strewn haphazardly across the mud. Tartan cloths, once vibrant, now lay muted and soaked through.

Angus, standing amidst the destruction, exhaled slowly. "The moors... they've seen storms before, but never like this. It's as if the very land weeps wi' us."

Fiona placed a hand over her heart. "Nature gives, but it also takes. We've seen its wrath today, but we'll find a way to rebuild. The Highlands, they teach us resilience."

Maree, her voice softer, turned to Dougal. "Elspeth warned us, Dougal, and we listened. Now, we rebuild, stronger than before."

Dougal nodded, but his face had gone pale. His gaze darted around the destruction, as if searching for something—or someone.

Off to the east, where the moorland rose into steep ridges, a trail of broken heather and blackened earth led away from the village—clear signs that something unnatural had passed that way. Fiona noticed it first, her breath catching as she pointed toward the distant hills. "Look... what manner of storm leaves a trail like that?"

Then, he turned to Maree, his voice low and urgent.

"Maree... where is Elspeth?"

MISSING ONE

The one person missing was Elspeth. Where had she gone? She had been there to greet Maree and Dougal upon their return, yet neither of them could recall whether she had been with them during the storm. It was as though she had vanished, carried away by the very winds that had torn through the Highlands.

Maree and Dougal, their hearts heavy with worry, took it upon themselves to search for her. They went from croft to croft, knocking on doors and asking their neighbours if anyone had seen the wise woman of the moors.

The villagers, still reeling from the aftermath of the storm, gathered in the village square. Concern etched every face as they realised Elspeth was nowhere to be found. It was as if she had been swallowed by the mist itself.

Angus, his brow furrowed, joined the search. "Elspeth has a way o' knowin' things, but this silence... it's unsettlin'. We need tae find her and learn what happened."

Fiona, a sense of foreboding in her eyes, added, "The storm and Elspeth's words, they were tied together. If she knew somethin' more, we must find her before the moors claim her secrets."

As they traversed the muddy paths, the Highland mist clung to them, thick with whispers that seemed to call from the past. The land, once peaceful, now felt heavy with unseen forces, as though the storm had awakened something old and restless.

The deeper they walked into the heather-covered hills, the more surreal their surroundings became. The mist curled like living tendrils around their legs, and every now and then, they heard faint echoes—whispers that sounded like their names, like old songs half-forgotten. The moors felt enchanted, or perhaps haunted, caught between what had been and what was yet to come.

It wasn't until they reached the outskirts of the village, near the ancient standing stones, that they found a clue. A tattered shawl, unmistakably belonging to Elspeth, clung to a thorny bush. The fabric was damp and frayed, as though it had been through the heart of the storm itself.

Maree picked it up, gripping the wool tightly in her hands. A chill ran down her spine. "She must have been here during the storm. But where is she now?"

Dougal, scanning the horizon, suddenly stiffened. "There!" He pointed toward a lone figure standing on the crest of the hill, barely visible through the lingering mist.

It was Elspeth.

She stood amidst the heather, her posture straight, her long grey hair unbound and whipping in the wind. She faced the moors with an unblinking stare, as though she were listening to something just beyond the reach of the living.

"Elspeth!" Dougal called, and the others followed suit, rushing toward her.

As they neared, she turned at last, her eyes filled with something unearthly—a wisdom that seemed to transcend time itself. Her skin was pale, her expression unreadable, and when she finally spoke, her voice was both reverent and heavy with meaning.

"I have communed wi' the winds, felt the very pulse o' the land as it cried out. The storm was nay just a storm, but a herald o' change. The moors are stirrin'. They speak o' a path yet unseen, a reckoning yet to come."

Maree, a mix of relief and unease in her voice, asked, "But where were ye, Elspeth? We searched everywhere."

Elspeth's gaze lingered on the ruined horizon, her voice lowering. "In the heart o' the tempest. While the winds howled and the earth trembled, I stood witness to the storm's true purpose. The moors, they are alive, and in their chaos, they reveal truths that mortals are oft too blind tae see."

Fiona shivered. "Elspeth... what did ye see?"

Elspeth took a deep breath, then whispered, "A shadow looms over the Highlands. It has nay yet taken form, but it is coming. This storm was only the beginning."

As her words faded into the mist, a strange silence fell over the stones. The standing circle, sacred for centuries, pulsed with an eerie stillness, as if holding its breath. Then, a single crow let out a cry from above, its wings slicing through the air as it took off into the grey sky—an omen, perhaps, of what still lay ahead.

A silence fell over them all, the wind carrying Elspeth's words into the vast moors. The villagers, now gathered around, felt the weight of what she had said.

And yet, though the storm had passed, its effects remained. The land bore its wounds—fallen trees sprawled across the moors, their roots torn from the soil, homes lay damaged, and fields that once promised a rich harvest now lay waterlogged and broken.

The people of the village did what Highlanders had always done—they worked. With sleeves rolled up and spirits unwilling to bend, they gathered in the square, dividing tasks among them.

"Ye take the north road an' help clear the paths!" shouted one of the men.

"We need strong arms tae fix the croft roofs!" called another, already hauling a fresh beam to replace one lost in the winds.

Children and elders alike joined in, collecting broken thatch, salvaging what they could from the wreckage. The villagers moved with purpose, but all the while, Elspeth's warning hung over them, unspoken yet felt by all.

Dougal worked alongside his neighbours, hauling timber, repairing fences, knowing full well that no storm—neither wind nor prophecy—would break the spirit of the Highlands.

Maree and Fiona worked together to prepare food for the weary. "The land'll heal," Maree murmured, glancing at the scarred moors beyond.

Fiona, ever perceptive, watched the villagers working. "Aye," she agreed, though her voice carried a quiet uncertainty. "But will we?"

That night, as they sat by the fire, Maree found herself staring into the flames. The heat on her face could not melt the unease in her chest. Dougal noticed her silence and wrapped an arm around her. "What is it, lass?" he asked. Maree shook her head. "Just... listenin'. I feel like the moors are still speakin'. But I cannae tell if they're warnin' us or grievin'."

It was then that a familiar voice broke through the hum of rebuilding.

"Well, it seems the ole home has taken a batterin'."

Maree turned, her breath catching as she saw Ewan and Morag approaching from the road.

Her older brother, once the heart of their family croft, now stood surveying the damage with the quiet reverence of a man who still felt its pull. Morag, his wife, rested a steadying hand on his arm, her keen eyes scanning the wreckage.

"We heard about dae storm," Ewan said, his gaze flickering to Maree before settling on Dougal. "Figured we'd better see how bad things were an' lend a hand."

Maree embraced her brother tightly, emotions tightening her throat. "It's bad, Ewan. Worse than we thought."

"Aye, but the village stands," he replied firmly, his voice grounding her in the same way it always had. "An' stand it always will."

Morag, ever practical, turned to Fiona. "We brought supplies—whatever we could gather. There's timber, food, an' some o' the men from our village will be along soon to help."

A wave of relief passed through them. Help had come—not just from within, but from those who had once called these lands home.

Fiona stepped forward and embraced Morag tightly. It was a rare gesture, one that spoke of old friendships and shared hardships. "We're glad to see ye," she said. "It means more than ye know." Around them, others greeted the new arrivals, hope slowly growing like fresh grass breaking through mud.

Elspeth, standing quietly nearby, nodded as if she had been expecting their arrival all along.

Maree turned back to her brother, tears prickling her eyes. "Thank ye, Ewan. It means everything."

Ewan clapped a hand on Dougal's shoulder. "Ye married into this land, Dougal, but now it's yours as much as it is ours. We'll rebuild together."

And so, the work continued, but with renewed strength, as old hands and new laboured side by side.

Elspeth watched them for a long while before murmuring, "Aye, the land will heal... but the storm was only the beginning."

Above them, the clouds had cleared, revealing a deep indigo sky scattered with stars. Yet one star pulsed brighter than the rest—strangely vibrant, as if keeping watch. Elspeth's gaze lingered on it. "There's still more to come," she whispered. "And the stars... they know it too."

The wind stirred through the moors, carrying her words into the distance, where something unseen waited.

TEMPEST WARNING

In the tempest of the mighty storm, Elspeth had been shown mysteries and events that were yet to unfold. Though the winds had settled and the sky had cleared, the echoes of the storm still whispered through the heather. The villagers gathered around her, eager to understand the cryptic words she had spoken upon her return.

Her eyes, distant and knowing, seemed fixed on something just beyond the veil of the present world. She stood near the great standing stones, the Highland mist curling around her like an ancient shroud. Her presence, ever commanding yet enigmatic, carried the weight of wisdom earned through time and something more—something otherworldly.

"The moors, ye see," she began, her voice steady yet heavy with meaning, "they're no' just land an' heather. They are a bridge between this world an' the next, a realm where the threads o' fate are woven by the winds themselves. In the heart o' the storm, I was shown glimpses o' what lies ahead."

The murmurs of the villagers quieted as they leaned in. Even the moors, it seemed, had hushed to listen. The mist thickened, wrapping around them in a silent embrace.

"I saw shadows an' echoes, symbols an' signs. The storm, it was a harbinger, a messenger from the very heart o' the Highlands. The land, it weeps, but it also prepares for a rebirth, a renewal born from the chaos."

Maree, standing close to Dougal, felt a shiver crawl up her spine. There was no doubt in her heart that Elspeth spoke the truth.

"What did ye see, Elspeth?" Maree's voice was quiet but insistent. "What do the moors foretell?"

Elspeth's hands, weathered by time and steeped in the magic of the Highlands, traced invisible patterns in the air as though weaving the story before their eyes.

"A journey lies ahead," she murmured, "a path woven wi' challenges an' choices. The threads o' yer lives are bound tighter now tae the moors, an' the storm has marked a crossroads, where destinies diverge."

A flicker of unease passed through the crowd. Even those who had long dismissed Elspeth's insights felt the gravity in her tone. The weight of prophecy clung to the air, heavy and tangible.

Dougal, ever the pragmatist, furrowed his brow. "Are ye sayin' we've more storms ahead? More trials?"

Elspeth's gaze drifted toward the distant hills, where the storm had left its scars upon the land.

"Storms, aye," she said, her voice laced with certainty. "But no' just those that rage in the sky. There are storms o' the spirit, storms o' the heart. An' some storms," she added, her voice dropping to a near whisper, "come walkin' in the shape o' men."

A hush fell over the gathering. The weight of her words settled into their bones like the mist clinging to the land.

Fiona, standing with her arms wrapped tightly around herself, asked the question that was thick on everyone's mind. "Then what are we tae do, Elspeth? If storms are comin', how do we face them?"

Elspeth turned, fixing Fiona with an unreadable gaze. "The winds may howl, an' the rains may pour, but within the chaos, there is a rhythm, a harmony that guides those who listen."

Somewhere in the distance, a curlew cried, its haunting call slicing through the mist like a warning. The villagers, already uneasy, turned toward the sound instinctively, as though even the birds sensed what was stirring.

A beat of silence passed before she continued. "We cannae control the winds or the storms," she said, her voice rising slightly, "but we can choose how we stand against them. The moors have spoken. Now, it is up tae each o' ye—listen, or be caught unaware."

With that, she stepped back, fading into the mist, leaving only questions in her wake.

Maree stood still, her breath shallow, her heart pounding with the weight of the revelation. She knew—Elspeth had not spoken everything. There was more to this story, more than the villagers had been given. And she also knew—she would have to find out what it was.

Not wanting to alarm Dougal or press Elspeth too soon, she kept her thoughts to herself, but the determination settled deep in her bones.

She needed to listen to the moors.

As the villagers dispersed, Maree lingered near the standing stones, her fingers grazing their rough surfaces. The Highland mist curled around her, whispering secrets only the wind could carry.

Dougal approached her then, quiet as the settling fog. "She spooks me, that one," he murmured. "Not because she's wrong... but because she's right too often." Maree gave a small nod, not looking away from the stones. "Aye," she said. "And sometimes, bein' right is the heaviest burden of all."

Dougal, sensing her unease, came to stand beside her. His presence was steady, grounding, but Maree could feel the tension in his stance.

"What do ye make o' Elspeth's words, lass?" he asked quietly.

Maree sighed, her breath clouding in the cool air. "I know there's more tae the tale than what she shared. The moors, Dougal... they've seen more than we can fathom. We need tae listen—to understand the language spoken by the winds an' the stones."

She bent down and picked up a piece of fallen heather, twirling it absently between her fingers. "The land remembers, Dougal. It remembers what we forget, what we bury, and what we fear. We just have tae be still long enough tae hear it speak."

Dougal was silent for a long moment before nodding. "Aye, there's wisdom in these hills, an' Elspeth kens it better than most. But are ye sure we can trust the moors tae guide us?"

Maree turned to him then, her gaze fierce but filled with something else—a quiet certainty that had not been there before.

"Trust, Dougal, is like the heather that carpets the moors—it grows slow, but once rooted, it endures. Elspeth may speak in riddles, but there's truth in her words. The moors... they are our compass, guidin' us through the storms an' the calm alike."

Dougal exhaled, the weight of the unknown settling upon them both. He wanted to believe her—wanted to trust the land that had given him a home, a family, and now a wife. But something gnawed at him, something unspoken.

They turned back toward the croft, but Maree knew in her heart—this was just the beginning.

The storm had marked a shift, a fracture in the world they knew, and she had no doubt that the winds of the moors had much more to tell.

TALES AND MYTHS

As Maree's understanding of the moors deepened, so too did her awareness that the Highlands carried stories far older than any living memory.

Some were written in books.

Most were not.

They lived instead in hearthside conversations, passed from one generation to the next like treasured heirlooms.

On quiet evenings, when the work of the day was done and the fire burned low, Maree often found herself remembering the stories her parents had told her as a child.

Especially her mother.

Arabella Doonagan had possessed a gift for storytelling.

She could turn an ordinary winter evening into an adventure simply by lowering her voice and leaning closer to the fire.

Maree smiled at the memory.

Many of those stories had terrified her.

Others had filled her with wonder.

And now, as she walked among the ancient standing stones, she found herself wondering whether some of them contained more truth than she had once believed.

The stones stood silent against the Highland sky.

Ancient.

Patient.

Watching.

She had visited them many times throughout her life.

Yet lately they felt different.

Not changed.

Awakened.

Or perhaps she was the one changing.

The wind moved through the heather, carrying familiar scents of earth and wildflowers.

Maree reached out and ran her fingers along the rough stone surface.

Generations had stood here before her.

Generations who had laughed, loved, mourned, and wondered about the same mysteries.

The thought humbled her.

As a child, she had listened wide-eyed to tales of the Feast of the Heather Moon.

Arabella claimed it had been celebrated long before anyone could remember.

Whether the festival had truly existed no one seemed entirely certain.

That never stopped the storytellers.

According to legend, Highland folk gathered beneath the midsummer moon carrying bundles of heather.

Fires blazed.

Music echoed across the hills.

Dancers moved beneath silver moonlight while elders offered blessings for the coming year.

The stories grew more elaborate with each retelling.

Some claimed hidden runes appeared within circles of heather.

Others insisted mysterious lights could be seen moving among the hills.

One tale spoke of a young woman who vanished after attempting to copy ancient symbols revealed beneath the full moon.

Maree had spent years peering suspiciously at every patch of heather she encountered afterward.

The memory made her laugh softly.

Children believed all sorts of things.

Yet the older she grew, the more she understood that such stories carried lessons beyond their surface.

The Highlands remembered.

That was what the elders always said.

The land remembered.

The people remembered.

Even when history itself forgot.

Other tales had spoken of creatures dwelling beyond ordinary sight.

The kelpies were among the most famous.

Arabella's version had always been particularly vivid.

She described magnificent horses rising from dark lochs beneath moonlight, their silver eyes gleaming as they watched the shoreline.

As a child, Maree had refused to go near water for an entire summer after hearing that story.

Her father had found this endlessly amusing.

Duncan, practical as ever, had spent weeks reassuring her that no water horses lurked behind every rock.

Though he always did so with a suspicious smile.

As if he wasn't entirely certain himself.

Then there was the bean-nighe.

The washerwoman of the ford.

That story had unsettled Maree far more than the kelpies ever had.

The image of a lonely figure washing bloodstained clothing in twilight shadows lingered long after the tale ended.

Even now she found herself glancing twice at mist-covered streams.

Old stories had a way of remaining with a person.

Especially Highland stories.

Yet it was the daoine sìth that fascinated her most.

Not because she believed every tale.

But because no two stories were ever the same.

Some described them as protectors.

Others as tricksters.

Still others spoke of ancient beings who moved through the hills unseen, guarding secrets older than memory.

Whenever Maree asked Elspeth about them, the old woman simply smiled.

"Some questions are better left unanswered, lass."

Which, of course, only made Maree more curious.

The standing stones rose around her.

Silent witnesses to centuries of stories.

Perhaps that was their true purpose.

Not portals.

Not gateways.

Not magic.

Memory.

The keeping of memory.

A way of reminding each generation that they belonged to something older than themselves.

A raven crossed the sky overhead.

Maree followed its flight until it disappeared beyond the hills.

The wind shifted.

A strange feeling settled over her once more.

The same feeling she had experienced increasingly often of late.

Not fear.

Not danger.

Expectation.

As though the land itself stood waiting.

Watching.

Listening.

"What are ye trying tae tell me?" she whispered.

The heather rustled softly around her.

No answer came.

At least not in words.

Yet deep within her, something stirred.

A sense that the stories she had loved as a child were not merely tales of the past.

They were threads.

And somehow those threads were leading toward something still unseen.

Maree stood quietly among the stones.

The Highlands stretched endlessly before her.

Ancient.

Beautiful.

Full of mysteries.

And for the first time, she felt as though she stood not at the end of a story, but at its beginning.

REBUILDING AMIDST THE MIST

The croft, nestled in the embrace of the moors, stood as a resilient witness to the aftermath of the worst storm in Highland history. The winds had howled, and the tempest had unleashed chaos, but now, as the mist began to lift, Maree and Dougal found themselves at the threshold of a new beginning.

"Look at the croft, Dougal. It's been through a lot, but it's still standin' strong," Maree murmured, brushing her fingers over the stone walls that had withstood both time and storm.

"Aye, lass. And we'll make it even stronger," Dougal replied, rolling up his sleeves, a determined grin playing on his lips.

The village, though battered and weary, echoed with the determined spirit of its people. The storm had left no home untouched, no croft unscathed, but neither had it broken them. Slowly, hammers rang through the moors, the scent of fresh-cut timber mingling with damp earth as repairs began.

Maree and Dougal took their place among the villagers, not just as newlyweds, but as part of the backbone of their home. The croft they shared would stand not only as their shelter but as a testament to resilience.

"Let's start wi' the beams," Dougal suggested, eyeing the damaged framework. "And maybe a wee kiss for good luck?"

Maree chuckled, swatting his arm. "Aye, for luck and a bit o' joy."

As they worked, they were not alone. Fiona and Angus arrived at dawn with extra timber and supplies, and the four of them worked side by side, the bonds between them strengthening with every nail driven into place.

"I dinnae think I'd ever be layin' bricks again," Angus admitted, wiping his brow, "but here we are."

Fiona, adjusting her scarf against the chill, smirked. "Ye're nae bad wi' a hammer, Angus MacLeod. Might keep ye around yet."

They rebuilt the barn roof together, sharing laughter between swings of the hammer. Maree, brushing windblown hair from her face, glanced at Fiona and said, "It's strange, is it no'? How a storm tears things apart, only tae bring folk closer." Fiona nodded, her smile tinged with something reflective. "Sometimes, it takes breakin' the roof tae open the sky."

By late afternoon, as the villagers were nearing the last of the major repairs, the sound of approaching hooves echoed through the village. Maree wiped the sweat from her brow and turned toward the familiar figures of Ewan and Morag, riding up the muddy path.

They had seen the destruction days ago, but returning now, they felt the full weight of what had been lost, and what still needed to be rebuilt.

Ewan swung down from his horse, his gaze settling on the repaired crofts and the villagers still working to mend what the storm had broken. "It's lookin' better than when we first laid eyes on it after the storm. Ye've all done well."

Morag, her sharp eyes scanning the village, nodded approvingly. "Aye, but there's still plenty left to be done. We talked it over, and we ken our place is here, helpin' put this village back on its feet. We've still got kin here, and this land—it's still ours as much as it ever was."

Maree smiled, the warmth of their words lifting some of the lingering exhaustion from her shoulders. "We need all the hands we can get. Ye're both welcome here, now and always."

Dougal clapped Ewan on the back, grinning. "Glad tae have ye back. There's no shortage o' work, that's for certain."

Morag rolled up her sleeves, eyeing the unfinished repairs around them. "Well then, let's get tae it."

With that, they rejoined the labour, their presence a quiet but powerful reassurance that no one would face the hardship alone.

Later, while carrying water from the well, Maree overheard young Callum asking his gran if the storm had been the end o' days. His gran chuckled and replied, "Nae, laddie. Just the end o' what needed endin'. Now we start again." It stayed with Maree, that thought—a Highland way o' seein' grief as part o' growin'.

That evening, with much of the heavy work done, the villagers gathered in the square to celebrate—a Highland tradition as old as the moors themselves.

Maree and Dougal, exhausted but content, welcomed their neighbours into their newly restored croft. The hearth crackled, its warmth seeping into the very bones of the home, casting golden light over tired but smiling faces.

Dougal raised a mug of heather ale, his voice carrying over the gathering. "Tae the moors that hae seen it a', and tae the bonds forged in their midst! Here's tae our village and the strength we find in each other!"

A chorus of cheers erupted, mugs clinking together, the echoes carried by the Highland wind.

The village square, which only days ago had been filled with debris and despair, now brimmed with laughter and music. Fiddles struck up a tune, the lively strains of a reel drawing villagers to dance, their feet kicking up the remnants of dust and mist.

Maree, watching the scene unfold, turned to Elspeth, who sat near the fire, her knowing eyes surveying the crowd.

"Elspeth," Maree said softly, "ye told us change was comin'. We never expected this."

Elspeth, wrapping her shawl tighter around her, nodded. "The storm didnae just test the village, lass—it reforged it. A storm clears what is weak so that only the strongest remains. And ye, Maree, are stronger than ye ken."

Maree swallowed, looking at her hands—calloused now from days of work, lined with dust and effort. She glanced at Dougal, who was laughing as he twirled a young lass in the dance, his face alive with unguarded joy.

"Aye," she murmured, more to herself than anyone else. "We all are."

Near the outer edge of the gathering, young Nessa recited a poem passed down from her grandmother, her voice light but clear as she stood on a rock. It spoke of storms and seedling growth, of hardship shaping roots. "If the wind bends ye, it doesnae mean ye're broken," she said, and the quiet that followed was filled wi' thought.

Fiona had been standing near the edge of the firelight, watching the dancers with a bemused smile. She'd been drawn into the joy of the night, but she had not expected to feel a hand suddenly take hers.

"Dance wi' me," Angus said, his voice quieter than usual, almost uncertain.

Fiona arched a brow, amused. "Ye? Dance?"

"Aye, well," he shrugged, tugging her gently into the open space. "I may be a wanderer, but even I ken the steps o' a reel."

Before she could protest, Angus spun her into the rhythm of the dance. They moved in time with the fiddles, their feet kicking up the damp earth as they joined the swirling revelry. Fiona laughed—a full, rich sound that Angus realised he liked hearing far too much.

As the music slowed for a moment, their steps naturally drew them closer. The firelight flickered against Fiona's face, her dark eyes searching his, and for a moment, Angus forgot everything else—the storm, the hardship, the uncertainty of what lay ahead.

"Ye look at me like ye've seen a ghost," Fiona teased, her voice softer now.

Angus swallowed, his grip tightening ever so slightly on her hand. "Nay, Fiona. I think I'm lookin' at somethin' real."

The air between them crackled, though not from the fire. Fiona parted her lips as if to say something, but before she could, Angus made the choice for both of them.

He kissed her.

It was gentle at first, uncertain, but when Fiona responded, her hands gripping his arms as though anchoring them both, the moment deepened. The music faded into the background, the village, the crowd—none of it mattered in that instant.

When they finally broke apart, Fiona chuckled, a breathless sound. "I didnae expect that."

Angus exhaled, his forehead resting lightly against hers. "Neither did I."

They did not need to say more. The moment had spoken for itself.

Elspeth moved quietly through the crowd, whispering blessings in Gaelic over each threshold, each hearth. "Let joy stay in this house, an' sorrow be light," she murmured. Her rituals, half-seen and wholly felt, were a thread of protection woven through the evening's joy.

As the night deepened, the Highland gathering became a tapestry of voices, stories, and music. The mist curled through the heather and ancient stones, carrying the laughter of the village into the vast expanse of the hills.

The storm had tested them, but it had not broken them. It had revealed their strength, their unity, and their will to endure.

And as the celebration stretched into the early hours, the echoes of joy, resilience, and love wove themselves into the very heart of the Highlands, leaving an indelible mark on the land that would long outlast the storm.

ANGUS'S ENIGMA

Amidst the lingering mist and the crackling hearth, Angus MacLeod found himself drawn deeper into the ever-unfolding Highland saga. The whispers of Elspeth, cryptic and laden with foresight, clung to the air like the last tendrils of a fading storm. Fiona, attuned to the ancient echoes of the Highlands, sensed that Angus carried a key—a key to something not yet fully understood.

"Fiona, lass, there's more tae me than meets the eye," Angus confessed, his gaze locked onto the distant moors as if seeking answers within their rolling expanse.

"Ah, Angus," Fiona murmured, watching him closely, "the moors are ancient keepers o' secrets. Let them guide us."

It was a quiet invitation, one that Angus, for reasons he didn't fully comprehend, felt compelled to accept.

So they walked—into the heather-clad hills, beyond the boundary of the croft, into the depths of the Highlands, where the standing stones loomed like sentinels of time itself. The mist parted before them, swirling like unseen spirits, beckoning them forward.

Fiona sensed the weight of untold stories pressing against Angus's soul. "The moors hae a language of their ain, Angus," she said gently. "If ye let yerself listen, they'll help ye find the words."

A moment passed. Then another. Finally, Angus exhaled.

"Here, Fiona, amidst the standin' stones, I'll share a fragment o' my tale," he said at last, resting a hand against the weathered surface of an ancient monolith. His voice, low and rough-edged, carried the weight of years.

He spoke of distant lands—of sunsets over the pyramids of Cairo, the bustling markets of the ancient city, the labyrinthine alleys where each step resonated with the echoes of pharaohs and the whispers of the Nile.

"In Cairo, Fiona, the air is thick wi' the scent o' history," he said, his voice tinged with something almost reverent. "The pyramids, they rise out o' the sands like giants, their stones older than the Highland hills. But it was nae just their grandeur that caught me—it was the carvings. Symbols, etchings... patterns etched into stone that felt strangely familiar. Too familiar."

Fiona tilted her head. "Familiar how?"

Angus let out a breath, shaking his head. "Because I'd seen them before. Here, in the Highlands." His fingers traced the carvings on the standing stone beside them, his touch lingering. "The same shapes. The same stories, told in symbols instead o' words. I thought at first it was coincidence, but the more I looked, the more I kent—it was somethin' more."

Fiona stared at him, captivated. "Ye think there's a connection? Between the Highlands and... Egypt?"

"Aye." His eyes darkened. "A thread that stretches farther than we can see. The pyramids, the standing stones—them that came before us kent somethin' we've forgotten."

The wind whistled between the stones, lifting Fiona's hair and sending a shiver through her. She had always believed the land carried memories, but to hear Angus speak of it this way, to suggest that their ancestors had known something vast and untold—it was unsettling.

And yet, she did not doubt him.

"What did it feel like?" she asked softly. "Standin' there, seein' it all wi' yer own eyes?"

Angus was quiet for a long moment, staring into the distance. When he spoke again, his voice was lower, rougher.

"Like standin' between two worlds, neither o' which I fully belonged to," he admitted. "Like I was seein' somethin' I was never meant tae see, yet somehow had always known was there."

Fiona reached out, hesitated, then rested a hand against his forearm.

"Ye belong here, Angus," she said quietly.

The words hit him harder than he expected.

For a man who had wandered more than he had ever stayed, who had left footprints in the sands of Egypt and along the riverbanks of the Amazon, the notion of belonging was foreign. Fleeting. A thing always just out of reach.

And yet, as he looked at Fiona, her dark eyes filled with quiet understanding, he felt something shift inside him.

He lifted his hand, covering hers. "Aye, maybe I do," he murmured.

A rare silence stretched between them, filled only by the sound of the wind and the rustling heather.

"Tell me more," Fiona urged after a while, as if sensing he needed the space to speak. "About the Amazon."

Angus let out a chuckle, shaking his head. "Och, Fiona, ye ask a man tae recount a lifetime."

"I've got time," she said, a small smile tugging at her lips.

So he told her. Of the Amazon's wild, untamed beauty. Of its endless green canopy, alive with creatures that few ever saw. Of the rivers that twisted like silver serpents through the land, carrying the lifeblood of an entire world.

"The air hums wi' life there," he said. "Ye can feel it in yer bones. It's as if the whole place breathes."

Fiona listened, enraptured, as he spoke of the jungle's symphony—the calls of howler monkeys at dawn, the shriek of macaws slicing through the sky, the whisper of unseen creatures moving just beyond the veil of leaves.

"I spent a year there, learnin' from the people who kent the land better than I ever could," Angus continued. "They showed me how tae read the signs in the trees, how tae track a jaguar just by the way the birds went quiet. It was a different kind o' wisdom than what we have here, but... it felt the same, somehow. Like the land itself was speakin', if only ye had the ears tae listen."

Fiona's fingers curled slightly against his arm. "And did ye listen, Angus?"

"Aye," he said, his voice quieter now. "And that's what brought me home."

He paused, then added, "But there was one night in the jungle I cannae forget. I saw lights, dancin' over the river. Not lanterns, no fire—just pure light, hoverin' like spirits. The elders called it a passage—when the veil grows thin. It felt... sacred."

Fiona's brows knit together. "Like the second sight?"

"Aye," he nodded slowly. "Only it was the jungle's version o' it. Their own kind o' seeing. I kent then that every land has its seers, its guardians. Elspeth is no' alone in what she feels."

Fiona looked out at the swirling mist, a reverence in her voice. "Maybe all the old places—here, the Amazon, even Egypt—they're just parts o' the same truth. Scattered, but connected."

Angus reached for her hand again, more certain this time. "An' maybe it's up tae us tae remember what's been forgotten."

Their eyes met then, something unspoken passing between them.

It was not a grand declaration. Not a confession of love, nor a sudden, breathless moment of passion.

But it was something.

A step toward something neither had fully acknowledged yet, but both had begun to understand.

Fiona exhaled slowly, glancing up at the sky, where the mist swirled in slow, endless spirals. "The moors," she said, "they've a way o' bringin' folk back to where they're meant tae be."

"Aye," Angus murmured, his fingers still resting against hers. "Aye, they do."

And as they stood among the ancient stones, surrounded by the land that had shaped them both, Angus MacLeod—wanderer, seeker, man of distant lands—felt, for the first time in a long time, that he had stopped running.

RETURN OF THE SIBLINGS

The Highland mist hung heavy in the air as Ewan, Isla, Fergus, and Caitriona, the Doonagan siblings, made their way back to the croft for a long-awaited reunion. Each step carried the weight of their varied experiences. The moors, ever watchful, seemed to welcome them with whispers of ancient kinship.

As they approached the croft, Maree, unaware of their impending arrival, tended to the hearth fire with Dougal by her side. The croft, usually echoing with the solitude of the moors, awaited the laughter and tales that the returning siblings would bring.

The door creaked open, and the siblings entered the warmth of the croft, their silhouettes flickering in the firelight. Maree, turning from the hearth, gasped in surprise. "Ewan, Isla, Fergus, Caitriona! What brings ye back tae the croft?"

Ewan stepped forward, a smile etched on his weathered face. "We heard o' the storm that threatened the village. Thought we'd come back an' share a moment wi' the family."

Isla chimed in, "Aye, Maree, the music o' the Highlands called us back home."

Fergus added, "The storm stirred the seas in more ways than one. When the moors roared, even the ocean seemed tae listen. I couldnae stay away."

Caitriona, her eyes filled with the wisdom of books and knowledge, nodded in agreement. "The tales of the moors reached us, and we couldnae resist the pull of home."

Maree, overwhelmed with joy, embraced each sibling in turn. The croft, once a haven for solitude, now echoed with the laughter and camaraderie of the Doonagan family.

The hearth fire crackled, casting dancing shadows on the walls of the croft as the Doonagan siblings gathered, their reunion echoing with the warmth of shared tales. Elspeth, ever the silent guardian, observed the scene with a knowing twinkle in her eyes.

Ewan, the stalwart elder, raised his mug and began, "The neighbouring village had its share o' challenges, but we faced them together. The Doonagan legacy stands strong."

"Aye, and the fiddle's found its way into the heart o' many a town," Isla said, her fingers tracing an imaginary melody in the air. "The Highland tunes—they bridge the miles between us an' this croft."

Fergus, with the sea breeze still clinging to his tales, chuckled. "The oceans tell stories, but none like the tales spun in the heart o' the moors. There's a kinship between the waves and these rolling hills."

Caitriona, the scholar among them, added, "Education has its treasures, but the truest wisdom lies in the whispers o' the moors. The croft's lessons echo through the pages of history."

Maree, her heart brimming with gratitude, turned to Dougal. "Dougal, love, our siblings bring the world tae our hearth. Their stories weave a rich tapestry, don't they?"

Dougal, a quiet observer in the midst of the familial exchange, nodded. "Aye, Maree. The moors have witnessed their journeys, and the hearth welcomes them home."

Elspeth, who had been silently watching, spoke in her gentle yet knowing voice. "The moors weave threads that bind family an' land. In their tales, ye find the heartbeat o' the Highlands."

Fergus leaned back in his chair, his gaze drifting toward the hearth. "Do ye remember when we used tae sneak out and follow the old stag trail up by the cairns?" he asked with a grin. "We swore we'd find the stone that sings at midnight."

Isla laughed, her voice bright as her fiddle's highest note. "Aye, and Ewan tripped in the burn, an' we all swore we'd seen the ghost o' the piper who vanished up the Glen."

Caitriona added thoughtfully, "Those stories we made up—they weren't just child's play. I think we were closer tae the truth of the moors then than we ever realised. There's somethin' ancient here, always listenin'."

Ewan's face grew sombre. "And what if it's no' just listenin' now, but callin'? The storm, the dreams... since it passed, I've had visions. Nothin' clear, just feelin's that the land remembers more than we do."

Maree nodded slowly. "Ye're no' alone in that. Sometimes I wake an' feel like the ground beneath the croft is whisperin' in a language I should understand, if only I'd stop tae listen."

Elspeth, her gaze fixed on the fire, added, "Aye, the land speaks—but it speaks in riddles. That's why the old stories matter. Ye may find the truth buried in the tale ye thought was jest."

As the firelight flickered, the siblings continued to share, their voices mingling with the ancient whispers of the croft. Elspeth's presence, a silent affirmation of the interconnectedness of past and present, seemed to infuse the room with an ageless wisdom that only the moors could hold. The Highland mist outside, enshrouding the landscape, embraced the croft and its occupants, sealing the bonds of kinship and heritage amidst the swirling tales of the Doonagan family.

Maree watched the flicker in Ewan's eyes, the sudden quiet that settled around Isla's fiddle. Something deeper lay beneath their words. "So why are ye really here?" she asked, her voice carrying a gentle insistence. The question hung for a moment, echoing the quiet anticipation of the moors.

Ewan exchanged glances with Isla, Fergus, and Caitriona. A solemn hush fell over the room before Ewan spoke, his gaze meeting Maree's. "The storm that swept through these lands, it wasnae just a tempest in the skies. There's a change in the wind, Maree, and we felt it in our bones."

Isla, her fingers absentmindedly playing with the strings of her fiddle, added, "The moors speak, and we've come tae listen. There's a tale unfoldin', and we're but threads woven into its fabric."

Fergus, usually buoyant with tales of maritime adventures, wore a contemplative expression. "The storm was a harbinger, Maree. It whispered secrets we've yet tae decipher, and the moors called us back tae do just that—together."

Caitriona interjected, "The croft, the moors—they're entwined in a story that goes beyond what meets the eye. We sensed a convergence... a juncture where the past an' future meet."

Maree, absorbing their words, felt a shiver run down her spine. The croft, usually a haven of warmth, now resonated with a sense of destiny. She glanced at Dougal, her partner in the dance of life, and saw in his eyes a reflection of her own questions.

Elspeth, the silent witness, spoke again, her words carrying a weight that transcended the room. "The moors have shown them glimpses, Maree. The storm left imprints on their hearts, and they've returned tae unravel the riddles woven into the Highland mist."

As the fire crackled and the Highland mist clung to the windows, the Doonagan siblings and Maree felt the weight of an unseen narrative, waiting to be unfolded amidst the moors' whispered secrets. The croft, steeped in the timeless wisdom of the Highlands, became a stage where the threads of fate and family converged, awaiting whatever tale the Highlands would reveal next.

A HIGHLAND TAPESTRY

As the fire crackled in the hearth, Ewan, the eldest of the Doonagan siblings, spoke of the responsibilities he shouldered in the neighbouring village. His weathered hands gestured with both pride and exhaustion as he recounted the daily toil of tending the land.

"Aye, the croft's doin' well enough," Ewan said, his voice rough with use. "But it comes wi' its burdens, tae. The crops thrive, and the beasts are healthy, but the land's never idle. It takes its toll, especially wi' the moor winds changin' the way they have."

Maree glanced toward Dougal, catching the curiosity in his expression. Ewan's wife, Morag, who hailed from another village, played no small part in keeping the croft running.

"And how's Morag?" Dougal asked, sincere interest in his voice.

Ewan traced invisible lines across the tabletop as he answered. The firelight danced across his features, softening the lines carved by wind and work. "Morag... she's the heart o' the place. Keeps the hearth warm and our spirits from saggin'. Couldnae do it without her."

He chuckled softly. "When the winters bite, and the wind howls like a banshee, she's the one makin' sure the fire never goes out. She's got a way wi' the flames, ye ken—turns even the coldest night into something near peaceful."

Dougal leaned in, drawn by the quiet reverence in Ewan's tone.

"And when the days stretch long and the work feels endless," Ewan went on, "it's her laugh that reminds me why we keep goin'. She's the soul o' that croft, Dougal. A light in the weary dark."

He looked up, meeting Dougal's gaze. "In her, I found a partner. No' just for the work, but for every storm we've ever weathered. We built that haven together, stone by stone."

Maree listened to Ewan's words, and in the firelight, she saw how much of herself and Dougal they reflected. A future, she thought, not just imagined, but built in moments like these. Quiet ones, full of truth.

As the warmth of Ewan's words settled in the room, Isla lifted her fiddle and let it sing. The notes spilt like clear water, weaving into the air with an ancient rhythm.

"The music, it's a lifeline," she said, fingers gliding over the strings. "Each tune's a thread in the weave o' the Highlands. Played in great halls, aye—and quiet places, too. But it always comes back tae this. Home."

Her eyes wandered toward the heather-lined paths outside the window. "Out in the wild, where the wind hums low, that's where I hear the old songs best. They come whisperin' through the stones, carryin' stories we're no' meant tae forget."

Elspeth gave a small nod from her corner seat, her eyes glinting. "Aye, lass. There's tunes ye play, an' there's tunes that play through ye. The old ones—those are the kind that find ye when the veil is thin."

The fiddle's song rose and fell, echoing the fire's crackle, drawing soft smiles from those around her.

As the melody faded, Fergus leaned back, a grin breaking across his weathered face.

"Ah, but ye should hear the sea when she's talkin'," he said. "Life on the water's a dance, right enough. The wind and waves—they've minds of their own. I've faced storms that'd tear the beard off a god, and calms so still it felt like breathin' wi' the world."

He gestured with wide hands. "The sea doesn't care who ye are. She humbles ye. And aye, she lifts ye, too. I've watched skies burn gold o'er the waves—colours ye cannae even name."

Caitriona smiled at that. "Sounds like the sea speaks poetry through ye, Fergus. Maybe ye've a bard's tongue an' never knew it."

The croft fell into a hush as he spoke, each listener swept along by the rhythm of his memories.

Then Caitriona, always more reserved, added her voice. "Books speak in whispers, too," she said softly. "In the quiet o' the library, I've heard the voices of those long gone. Wisdom passed down, waiting tae be picked up again."

She looked around the room, her gaze thoughtful. "These hills, these stones—they've stories that dinnae fit neatly on a page. But they're there, written in the wind, in the lichen on the standing stones. The moors remember."

She glanced toward the fire. "In teachin' others, I've come tae understand that. It's no' just knowledge—it's legacy. It's belonging."

Isla leaned her fiddle gently against her chair and reached across the table to clasp Caitriona's hand. "We each bring a thread, don't we? The land, the song, the sea, the page. All part o' the same weave. I reckon that's what brings us home."

The flicker of the hearth caught in everyone's eyes as her words settled among them.

Dougal sat quietly, absorbing it all. For so long, he'd wandered alone, following paths that never quite led home. But here, in the croft filled with stories and song, something had changed. He saw the way Maree leaned into the warmth of her family, and how they leaned back.

And for the first time in years, he felt not like a guest, but a thread in the weave.

Maree squeezed his hand. Across the fire, Elspeth's watchful gaze held its own quiet blessing.

Elspeth's voice, usually reserved, rose once more as she looked around the gathered faces. "The moors remember when families gather, when tales are shared, an' hearts are mended. This night—ye'll no forget it. An' neither will the land."

The moors stirred outside, soft and vast and listening.

And within the croft, the stories burned bright.

CAITRIONA'S DISCOVERY

In the quiet corners of the croft, where the shadows danced in tandem with the flickering hearth fire, Caitriona found herself immersed in the world of dusty tomes and weathered manuscripts. Her pursuit of knowledge had taken her beyond the croft and into the realm of literature and history. As the winds whispered through the pages of forgotten legends, Caitriona stumbled upon a tale that seemed to resonate with the very heartbeat of the moors.

The legend, buried deep in the annals of Highland history, spoke of a time when the moors were not just a patch of land but a tapestry woven with threads of magic and mystery. It narrated the stories of ancient guardians, beings of ethereal grace, who were said to have watched over the Highland landscape since time immemorial. Their existence, like the mist that clung to the moors, was veiled in secrecy, known only to those who dared to delve into the forgotten lore.

As Caitriona unravelled the tale, she discovered subtle connections between the legend and the mysteries Elspeth had alluded to after the tempest. The ancient guardians, it seemed, were intertwined with the very essence of the land, their presence a silent but potent force shaping the destiny of those who tread upon the Highland soil.

Her fingers trembled as she turned the brittle pages, each word seeming to echo with quiet urgency. This wasn't just history—it was a mirror to the unease they all felt in the storm's wake. The moors weren't finished speaking.

Eager to share her findings with the family, Caitriona gathered them around the hearth fire. The flames cast dancing shadows on the walls as she recounted the forgotten legend, her words carrying the weight of centuries. The siblings listened with bated breath, and even Dougal, with his wandering spirit, felt a sense of anticipation in the air.

She opened the book carefully, turning it toward Maree. "Here—it says the guardians revealed themselves only when the land was threatened. That's why the storm matters—it stirred what was buried. It's happened before, and it's happenin' again."

"It speaks of a hidden path," Caitriona said, her voice low but certain. "A journey for those with Highland blood an' Highland hearts. It promises truths that'll bridge the past and present. Secrets lingerin' just beyond the veil."

Elspeth, the woman of the mist, nodded knowingly. "The journey begins where the ancient stones stand sentinel," she said. "Their whispers'll guide those who dare tae listen."

Maree, her heart entwined with the land, looked from face to face. "We're treadin' sacred ground, we are. And I feel it in my bones—we're meant tae find what's been buried."

Fergus leaned forward, pointing to a sketched map in the manuscript. "This looks like the northern ridge near Brannoch Hill. I fished near there once—there's a cave system hidden by the gorse. Ye think the path starts there?"

The croft, surrounded by the ever-watchful moors, became the starting point of their mystical odyssey. The ancient stones, weathered by time, stood as witnesses to the gathering—a silent chorus awaiting the first steps of a journey that would lead them to the heart of Highland mysteries.

* * *

In the days that followed, the family delved into the lore of the ancient guardians, each member bringing something unique. Elspeth shared fragments of old Gaelic chants, passed down through generations, said to stir the magic still sleeping in the soil. Fergus, with his keen eye for the stars, noted alignments in the night sky that matched tales found in the pages Caitriona unearthed.

Isla, caught up in the enchantment of it all, composed a melody that seemed to echo back at her when played near the stones. "Music remembers what minds forget," she'd said, tuning her fiddle by the fire.

Ewan, whose strength usually lay in toil, surprised them all by carving replicas of the symbols they found in the manuscript. "I dinnae ken much about books, but I learn wi' my hands," he said, as he etched a spiral into a stone amulet. "This one—this feels important."

Ever the practical one, Ewan studied the flora and fauna of the moors, marking changes, listenin' for signs in the land. "Nature keeps her own records," he muttered, scribblin' in his journal.

Dougal, still adjusting to life with the family, found himself watching it all with quiet reverence. The storm had shifted something in him—not just fear, but love. When Elspeth vanished, the thought of losing them all had landed heavy. He'd found something here—something worth protecting.

Fiona brought with her a bundle of old prayer beads said to have belonged to a nun who lived in the glen centuries before. "She was called the Listening Sister. Folk said she could hear the land sigh in her sleep," Fiona said. "These might help us hear, too."

Their preparations took them to the ancient stones—weathered sentinels, watching without judgment. The family stood together, each of them holding a piece of the riddle.

Elspeth raised her hands, her voice deep and melodic, chanting words older than any they'd heard. The air crackled. The stones glowed. The path lit itself before them like the land was breathing in light.

For a heartbeat, Maree saw something—a tall, glimmering figure just beyond the last stone, cloaked in mist and moonlight. It raised no hand, spoke no words. But its presence... it felt like a blessing, or a warning.

As they stepped forward, the moors whispered, and the wind carried Isla's song far beyond the hills.

The journey into the heart of Highland mysteries had begun. The croft, now wrapped in anticipation, awaited their return. For the moors had called them—and they had answered.

THE ROCKS CRY OUT

The ancient standing stones, weathered and adorned with mystical etchings, stood as silent storytellers of Highland secrets. The symbols etched into the stones formed an intricate tapestry, a treasure map woven with threads of destiny. As the Doonagan family gathered around these weathered sentinels, they traced the patterns with eager fingers, seeking clues to the mysteries that lay ahead.

The symbols told of a hidden path, marked by the dance of ancient guardians and the whispers of the moors. Spirals spoke of cyclical journeys, knots represented intertwined fates, and crescent moons hinted at the mystical power that waxed and waned with the Highland tides. Each family member, in the flickering light of the hearth fire, contemplated the etchings, wondering if they truly held the key to the revelations they sought.

Yet, amidst the enthusiasm, a shadow of uncertainty lingered. Ewan, deeply rooted in his neighbouring village, glanced at his siblings, thinking of his wife and weighing the cost of this venture on the life he had built. Isla, a free spirit enchanted by the melodies of distant towns, wondered if the journey would pull her too far from the music she loved. Fergus, the adventurer, felt the call of the sea echoing in his soul, torn between the maritime tales of the past and the mysteries unfolding before him. Caitriona, the scholar, embraced the knowledge but pondered the sacrifices it might demand.

Even Dougal, the wandering soul finding solace in the family's embrace, questioned if he was prepared for a journey that reached beyond the physical landscapes he'd roamed. Elspeth, her eyes veiled in ancient wisdom, observed the family dynamics, knowing that the path ahead held both revelations and challenges.

Maree knelt before one of the stones, her fingertips tracing a spiral that shimmered faintly in the fading light. "It's like the land itself remembers," she whispered. "And it wants us tae remember too."

As they stood before the etched stones, the Doonagan family, bound by blood and purpose, faced not only the mysteries of the moors but also the uncharted territories of their own hearts. The symbols on the stones beckoned them forward, promising a journey that would weave their destinies into the very fabric of the Highland tapestry.

Ewan, his gaze lingering on the etchings of the ancient stones, pondered the implications of the journey. Beside him, Maree, still in the bloom of newlywed bliss, felt a mixture of excitement and trepidation.

"Dougal," Maree said, her voice soft in the Highland air, "what d'ye make o' these symbols? Do they hold the truths Elspeth spoke of, or are they just the fancy scratchin's of ancient hands?"

Dougal, tracing the patterns with a contemplative hand, replied, "Och, the moors speak in ways we dinnae always ken. These stones—aye, they've seen a lot. I reckon there's more tae 'em than meets the eye."

The siblings exchanged glances, shared curiosity flickering between them. Caitriona stepped forward, her eyes bright with purpose.

"The lore I found speaks of guardians," she said, "beings of light and grace. They're said tae guard the secrets of the moors—protectors of a path that winds through time and fate."

Isla gave a cheeky grin. "A hidden path, ye say? I've played tunes for all kinds of folk, but this might be the grandest stage yet."

Fergus crossed his arms, nodding. "Be it storm or spell, the moors are callin'. I say we follow. Adventure's always been my compass."

Ewan looked to Maree and Dougal, then back to the others. "We've weathered storms together. Whatever this is, we face it as kin—bound by blood an' purpose."

"And by the land itself," added Elspeth, stepping forward. "It's no accident the stones called to ye. Ye're part of somethin' older than any of us—older than the hills."

As they studied the stones, a soft hum rose, vibrating the air. The symbols shimmered faintly. Elspeth stepped closer, whispering in a tongue older than the hills.

The earth groaned. Stones shifted. A hidden stairway unfurled beneath their feet.

They all stared.

"Well," Ewan muttered, voice low with wonder, "the path is open. The rocks cry out wi' tales yet tae be told. Let's no' turn back now."

With shared resolve, the Doonagans descended into the unknown.

The stairway opened into a mist-filled corridor, glowing with an otherworldly sheen. Elspeth led the way, her lantern a flicker in the shimmering dark.

Along the corridor walls, ancient murals appeared—depictions of Highland clans standing beside otherworldly beings, their arms raised together against an unseen force. Fergus paused. "These folk look like us," he whispered. "But... different. Changed."

The mist parted now and again, revealing fleeting visions—floating stones, glowing runes, and winds that seemed to whisper names. Time felt elastic, moments stretching and folding like breath.

Ewan, Maree, Isla, Fergus, Caitriona, and Dougal walked through this ever-shifting dreamscape, guided by the hum of ancient magic.

At the end of the path, a glowing archway formed from mist. Elspeth turned.

"Beyond this gate lies the heart o' the Highland mysteries," she said. "Each of ye will be tested. Some answers ye'll expect. Others—ye won't. But trust in what binds ye. It's stronger than ye think."

The family stepped through.

What met them was no ordinary realm. They found themselves in a land that shimmered like memory.

Ewan stood at the edge of a windswept cliff. On the far side of a deep chasm, ghostly ancestors watched. They didn't judge. They waited. He understood then: his role wasn't tae lead alone, but tae protect, to hold the door open for those to come.

Maree wandered a heathered field. The colours shifted with her thoughts—flashes of Dougal, of storms survived, of love deep as roots. She pressed a hand to her chest. The land answered back.

Isla danced beneath a sky swirling with notes—tunes she'd never played, yet knew by heart. Spirits whirled around her, bowing to her rhythm.

Fergus sailed across seas conjured from memory, wind in his hair, the scent of salt and ash on the air. Each wave was a choice, each crest a lesson.

Caitriona stood in a vast library where books opened themselves. Symbols floated before her eyes, ancient and glowing. She read not with her mind, but with her heart.

Dougal walked paths he had once travelled. Each land-mark whispered a truth: belonging isn't about place, but about who you walk beside.

And still, Elspeth watched them all from a distance—her form flickering between shadow and starlight. She whispered blessings beneath her breath, shaping protections that only the moors could understand.

Eventually, their paths led to a starlit clearing. A still pool mirrored the sky.

Elspeth appeared. "Ye've walked through fire an' fog. The moors have marked ye. What ye carry now—is no just memory. It's magic."

She lifted her hands. The winds stirred.

"The rocks cried out, an' ye answered. Now carry it forward. The land has gifted ye a piece o' itself."

The clearing dissolved into light.

They were back beneath the standing stones. The Altar of the Highland Veil glowed behind them.

The moors whispered.

"Ye've seen what lies hidden," Elspeth said quietly. "But the tale's no' done. Not by a long shot."

Ewan placed a hand on the altar. "Then let's keep goin'. We've come too far tae turn back."

A tune rose on the wind.

Isla tilted her head. "That melody again. It's callin' us."

Ewan nodded. "Aye. Let's see where it leads."

They walked into the moors, the land unfolding like a story.

Glens opened before them like secrets. Moss-covered ruins whispered old rites. Lochs shimmered with starlight. The moors weren't just landscape—they were memory, song, breath.

At a fork in the trail, a lone stag stood, watching them. Its eyes glowed faintly golden. Caitriona stilled, her breath catching. "A sign," she murmured. "Or a warning." The stag bowed its head, then vanished into the mist.

* * *

Elspeth appeared now and then, a shadow in the mist, leaving them riddles more than answers.

At the shore of a quiet loch, she said, "This is a turning. The moors have brought ye here for a reason. Pay heed."

The Doonagans stood quiet, watching the sky shift on the water.

Far away, clouds gathered again. The wind changed.

The moors held their breath.

A storm was coming—but not just of wind and rain.

A reckoning.

And deep beneath the stones they'd left behind, something ancient stirred. Something that had waited long enough.

And the family, hearts bound to the land, would be ready.

Whatever came next, they would face it together.

THE RECKONING
TEMPEST

The first inkling of the impending tempest manifested in the subtle shift of the wind's melody. The air, once gentle and familiar, now carried an undercurrent of restless energy. Elspeth, attuned to the nuances of the moors, felt the change in the wind's whispers and furrowed her brow in silent contemplation.

Ewan, feeling the urgency in the shifting winds, swiftly mounted a horse and galloped to the next village to gather his wife, Morag, and a few essential belongings. Morag, seemingly anticipating his arrival, had already packed some gear, and her lack of surprise was evident when Ewan rode up.

"A storm brewin' already?" she asked, handing him a sack.

"Aye," Ewan said, swinging it onto the saddle. "An' it's no small one either. Come on, lass—we've nae time tae waste."

A quick kiss and a tight hug later, they gathered their things and rode hard for the croft.

Back at the croft, Isla and Caitriona were gathering herbs and dried foodstuffs, their movements practised and swift. Isla, her brow furrowed, muttered, "This storm's carryin' more than rain. There's a weight in the wind I dinnae like." Caitriona nodded, tucking a pouch into her satchel. "It's a reckoning, Isla. The kind that changes stories."

* * *

Upon their return, Ewan's siblings—along with Fiona, Angus, Dougal, and Elspeth—had been actively assisting the rest of the village in preparing for the deluge. A palpable tension hung in the air as the villagers, united by the approaching tempest, moved with a shared purpose. Horses, stalwart companions of the Highland crofts, were led to the safety of barns. Tethered within the warmth of familiar walls, they shifted nervously, sensing the imminent tumult.

Guided by years of communal wisdom, the villagers worked tirelessly to secure their homes and belongings. Barrels, tools, and precious possessions were tied down or sheltered. The crofters moved with a diligence born of necessity, every gesture steeped in a quiet prayer to minimise what the storm might take.

As the first gusts of wind heralded the storm's arrival, the village stood as a testament to the resilience of Highland communities. Unity became a shield against the elemental forces that tested their bonds. In hushed tones, the impending deluge brought forth a resolve forged by generations.

The sky darkened as clouds gathered in an ominous congregation. The wind, once a murmur, began to keen through the valleys. Leaves swirled across the moors, and the distant roar of the sea rose with eerie insistence.

In the midst of preparation, the hopes, dreams, and prayers of the village converged. Each crofter, with weathered hands and steadfast determination, sent silent entreaties to the moors. The Highland mist, thickening in response to the atmospheric turmoil, seemed to echo those unspoken pleas.

Inside the croft, Maree lit a fresh taper from the hearth and placed it beside the stone carved with their family crest. "For strength," she whispered, "an' for those who came before." Fergus entered behind her, carrying armfuls of dry wood. "We'll need all the blessings we can get."

The air buzzed with something greater than wind—it was the heartbeat of a people standing together. In the heart of the village, the croft of Maree and Dougal became a microcosm of this spirit, glowing with quiet strength.

Some raindrops fell, and a hush settled over the land, broken only by the distant growl of thunder. The villagers, heads bowed against the wind, stood united in quiet determination. The moors had seen their kind through many trials. They would not falter now.

The winds roared like a wild beast, tearing through the moors with relentless force. Gusts carried tales from the Highland past—a symphony of howling spirits and ancient grief. Trees groaned under the strain, their branches flailing in chaotic frenzy.

The sea surged in storm-fuelled fury, crashing against the cliffs in a deafening cadence. Once serene waters turned violent, echoing the storm's primal howl.

In the village, crofts stood resilient, but not untouched. Roofs were torn loose and hurled into the darkness. The rain fell in torrents, churning the land into shifting mud. The air was thick with heather, earth, and the salt of the storm-driven sea. Mist swirled in ghostly patterns, cloaking the village in an otherworldly veil.

Among the chaos, villagers toiled without rest. Hammer strikes, creaking timber, and urgent voices rose in defiance of the storm's rhythm.

"Watch that beam, Dougal!" Fergus shouted, straining to hold it steady.

"Aye, I've got it!" Dougal yelled back, teeth gritted. "This wall's no' comin' down if I've got any say in it!"

Elspeth moved silently through it all, barefoot on the sodden ground. Arms lifted, she seemed to draw strength from the very bones of the earth. Lightning cracked overhead, illuminating her silhouette—a sentinel against the storm.

Somewhere near the stone circle, Angus wrestled a canvas tarp over the livestock shelter. Fiona appeared beside him with ropes, soaked to the bone but fierce. "They're frightened, Angus," she said over the wind. "Like they know this isnae just weather." He glanced at her, the storm reflected in his eyes. "Aye. The land's cryin' somethin' ancient."

The tempest carved its tale across the land, a tapestry of destruction and resilience. When the fury ebbed, it left behind a moor transformed—and a village that had endured.

But even as calm returned, something restless lingered.

As the storm rolled in once more, anticipation weighed heavy. The Doonagan siblings—Maree, Dougal, Angus, Fiona, and Elspeth—each felt the shift in the air. The Highland mist coiled low, preparing to shroud the moors.

Maree, brows drawn, stared through the window. "Another storm... so soon? What more can it bring, I wonder?"

Dougal stepped up beside her, eyes on the horizon. "The moors have their own way o' speakin', lass. Let's hope this one brings answers instead o' ruin."

Elspeth stood once more in communion with the elements. Her eyes reflected the wild, knowing wisdom of the land. The winds spoke, and she listened.

Angus, broad shoulders braced against the cold air, murmured, "The moors are hummin' wi' tales. Maybe this storm's here tae speak truths we've forgotten."

Fiona glanced toward him, calm and certain. "Whatever it is—we face it together. The moors test us, aye. But they pull us tighter too."

Elspeth moved through the village at twilight, a pouch of herbs in hand. She scattered them at doorsteps and murmured protection charms in Gaelic. The children peeked through shutters as her soft chanting floated past. "A storm that speaks carries more than rain," she whispered. "It carries memory."

As the mist thickened, the croft glowed warm from within. The firelight flickered in patterns that mirrored the dance of wind outside. The siblings gathered, the croft becoming both refuge and rally point.

The villagers, seasoned by past storms, stood shoulder to shoulder. They secured what they could, speaking few words. The storm's song grew louder.

Ancient stones hummed beneath the earth. The moors whispered secrets lost to memory. The Highland spirit did not waver.

In the heart of the moors, Elspeth stood once more at the eye, her presence a stillness amid the chaos. The storm, as foretold, revealed more than destruction—it unveiled.

And the moors, cloaked in mist, stood watchful and waiting—knowing the storm had not ended, only changed form.

FIONA'S VISION

In the aftermath of the tempest, as the Highland mist slowly began to lift, the Doonagan family gathered in the warmth of their croft, seeking solace and understanding. Fiona, ever attuned to the whispers of the moors, felt the weight of the recent storm resonate with a deeper cosmic pull. Her intuitive gifts, a conduit between the seen and unseen, stirred with heightened sensitivity.

Seated by the hearth, the family turned to Fiona, their eyes reflecting a mix of curiosity and trepidation. Angus, too, leaned in, his rugged features softened by quiet anticipation. Elspeth, the woman of the mist, sat in contemplative silence, her gaze fixed on the flickering flames, as if deciphering the remnants of ancient messages embedded in the fire's dance.

Fiona, her eyes distant, began to share the visions that had unfolded in the recesses of her mind. "The moors... they're ancient storytellers, aye? Weavin' tales that stretch far past what we can see. In the storm's fury, they were speakin'—showin' threads of destiny that tie us right tae this land."

She spoke of an intricate dance between nature's forces and the lives entwined with the Highland moors. The storms, she said, were no mere weather. "They're echoes, ken? Echoes of somethin' far older. It's no just rain an' wind—it's a call, a message sent in breath an' thunder."

Her voice dropped, hushed. "I saw the heather ablaze wi' light—not fire, no, but a glow from the auld world. Shapes moved between the stones—not ghosts, but memories. An' at the centre... a doorway o' mist, breathin' like a livin' thing... waitin'."

The family listened in silence. Even the fire seemed to pause, its crackle holding its breath.

"The moors want us tae listen," Fiona said. "An' in return, they'll show us pieces o' what's tae come. But only if we dare tae look."

She paused, her eyes narrowing slightly as if focusing on something just beyond the edge of sight. "I saw a stag—tall and burnished wi' light—standin' at the cairn beyond the Rowan woods. Its eyes met mine, and I kent it was no beast, but a messenger. A guardian."

"A guardian o' what?" Caitriona asked, barely above a whisper.

"Of a path we've yet tae find," Fiona replied. "But we're bein' beckoned, one by one. That stag, it's the first sign. There'll be others. We need tae be watchin'."

Morag shifted uneasily beside Ewan. "If the moors are stirrin' and sendin' signs, we cannae afford tae miss them. We'll need more than strength—we'll need unity."

"Then we make ready," Maree said, her voice steady. "Whatever this change is, it's comin' through us, and we need tae be open—heart, mind, an' soul."

Fiona looked to Elspeth, who gave a slow nod. "Aye," Elspeth said. "The land's already chosen its storytellers. We're no' just hearin' the tale—we're bein' written into it."

The weight of her words settled over the room. Maree, her brow furrowed, turned to Elspeth. "What are the moors tryin' tae tell us? Why storms like that? We're here. We're listenin'. So what's it all mean, Elspeth?"

Elspeth's features, lined by years and quiet knowing, were calm. "The storms speak, lass. In the dialect of auld winds. The moors are stirrin'. They're sharin' their tale, bit by bit. But tae hear it proper, we'll have tae go deeper—deeper into the mist, where truth hides and waits."

The siblings exchanged glances. A silence heavier than before wrapped around them like fog on the moors. Ewan, Morag, Isla, Fergus, and Caitriona all bore the same furrowed look.

Ewan broke the still. "We've weathered many a storm, but this... this one felt like it was speakin'. An' we've nae got the words for it. Not yet."

Isla nodded. "The music's always guided me. But now? It's like the tune's shifted. We've lost the harmony."

Fergus leaned forward, jaw tight. "I've been through tempests at sea. None like this. It felt... personal. Like the land itself was cryin' out."

Caitriona's tone was quiet, but sure. "In all my reading, all the lore—I've found nothin' like this. It's like the past has gone silent, and only the land remembers."

Maree turned back to Elspeth. "Ye've lived longer wi' these moors than any of us. What do ye feel in yer bones?"

Elspeth didn't hesitate. "The moors are risin'. Their whispers are louder now. But what they speak—it's no' for ears. It's for the soul."

Angus, who had listened quietly, finally spoke. "There's a hum. A kind o' resonance in the land. Maybe we need tae tune ourselves tae it. No just listen—align."

The croft, once their comfort, now held a strange hush. Outside, mist passed across the windowpane like a pale hand. The fire popped, sending up a flicker of sparks.

Fiona, voice low, eyes unfixed, murmured, "There's a birth in the chaos. The moors are sheddin' the old ways. What's comin'... it's a transformation. An' we're part of it."

Elspeth gave a solemn nod. "Aye. The land lives in cycles. This storm—it wasnae just destroyin'. It was clearin' the way. What comes next depends on how we answer."

Morag, who'd stayed quiet, looked to Ewan. "Then we best be ready tae answer true."

Maree stepped forward, steady. "What must we do, Elspeth?"

Elspeth's gaze turned toward the window, where mist kissed the glass. "Listen, lass. Listen wi' yer whole self. There's a cairn beyond the Rowan woods—old, near forgotten. Go when the mist returns. It'll speak clearer than I ever could."

The croft held its breath.

Surrounded by the storm's lingering weight, the Doonagan kin stood united. Their hearts, bound by blood and the pulse of the Highlands, leaned in toward the silence beyond. And outside, the moors—ever watchful—waited.

THE HEARTH GROWS

The morning mist curled low around the moors, rising in soft ribbons from the heather as if the land itself were sighing. Maree stood barefoot in the garden behind the croft, her hands buried in the cool earth. The storm had passed, but something in the air still shimmered—like breath held just before a song. Birds had returned to the hedgerows. Wildflowers, flattened by rain, reached upward again.

From within the croft, the soft clatter of dishes and the low murmur of voices signalled that the others were stirring. The house was full again. And yet, Maree felt the need to speak, not just to her family, but to the land that had shaped them.

She walked inside, wiping her hands on her apron, and found them gathered around the hearth—Ewan, Isla, Fergus, Caitriona, Angus, Morag, Dougal, Fiona, and Elspeth. They had been laughing moments ago, but something in Maree's expression stilled them.

She stepped forward, voice calm but full of conviction. "It's time to come home, my brothers and sisters. The Highlands are callin', and it's not just in the wind or the soil. It's in us. The storm cleared more than the skies. It showed us that every one of us is needed here now. Each of us holds a thread in this tapestry."

There was a silence, not of discomfort, but of reverence. The crackle of the hearth filled the pause.

Ewan, hands clasped before him, nodded slowly. "The croft welcomes ye all. There's work ahead—but good work. Purposeful work."

Isla smiled. "The music of the Highlands has a new melody. Maybe it's time I stayed still long enough to listen to it fully."

Fergus leaned back, a flicker of uncertainty in his gaze. "I've wandered the seas all my life. And maybe I always will. But this place... it sings to somethin' deeper than saltwater."

Caitriona folded her hands in her lap. "The libraries can wait. What we're building here—it's a living history."

Angus looked out the window at the mist hugging the stones. "The moors keep secrets, aye—but maybe they're ready to share, if we plant ourselves deep enough."

Even Dougal, still adjusting to the weight of so many voices after a life of solitude, added, "Never thought I'd settle. But this—this doesn't feel like settlin'. It feels like answerin'."

Only Elspeth said nothing. But her eyes shimmered with knowing.

Fiona stepped forward, her voice gentle. "The moors led me here for a reason. I always thought I was just passin' through—but now, I ken I'm meant tae stay. This land—this family—it anchors me."

Morag clasped Maree's hand, her voice filled with quiet resolve. "I've stood by Ewan through many seasons. But here... here feels like the place where the roots take hold. I'm ready to help tend this soil."

Caitriona, thoughtful as ever, glanced toward the stone walls. "What if we built a library right here? A place for the young ones—and the old—to learn from the past while dreamin' o' the future?"

Isla, eyes gleaming, added, "And a music house. A ceilidh space where folk can gather an' sing the songs o' their hearts."

Fergus raised an eyebrow. "If ye're buildin' all that, I'll need a workshop. I've got ideas for tools an' sails that might just keep the winds o' change blowin' the right way."

And so, in the days that followed, they built.

Ewan, Dougal, and Fergus raised walls with calloused hands and careful precision. Morag, with quiet grace, brought warmth and rhythm to each new space. The croft that had once sheltered only Maree and Dougal grew into a cluster of homes—each one humming with life.

Maree and Morag shared not just the kitchen, but the joy of simple tasks—kneading dough, preserving jams, hanging herbs from wooden beams. Their laughter wove through the rafters like a second kind of smoke.

Caitriona rode off one crisp morning, a promise to return on her lips. Weeks later she did—books strapped to her saddle, scrolls tucked under her arms, knowledge spilling from her like spring rain.

Isla's return was less quiet. Her buggy rattled with instruments from every corner of the country. Within days, the croft sang. Fiddle tunes. Harp chords.

Droning whistles at dusk. Music that seemed to rise from the earth itself.

Fergus brought stories from ports and places the others had never seen—strange legends, spices for the stew pot, and an uncanny knack for fixing what was broken.

Elspeth tended a small grove just beyond the garden, planting rare herbs under moonlight. "These," she whispered to Maree, "are for times yet tae come. They'll know when they're needed."

As the crofts rose, so too did their sense of rootedness. Paths were worn into the grass between houses. Lanterns lit the way from one hearth to another. The moors, once solemn observers, seemed to smile in the golden hush of evening.

One night, after the last of the beams had been raised, they gathered around a shared fire. Isla played a soft tune.

Fergus passed around a dram. Maree leaned into Dougal, her hand resting on her belly—a quiet promise of the future.

Elspeth stood at the edge of the firelight. "The moors have seen many come and go," she said. "But it's been long since they watched a family grow like this. You've built more than homes. You've built harmony."

And for a long while, no one spoke. They only listened—to the music, to the wind, to the moors. The hearth had grown. And so had they.

CALL OF THE ANCIENTS

The Highland mist lingered softly over the moors, golden in the early light, wrapping the land in a hush that felt holy. Smoke curled gently from the chimneys of the crofts, and laughter carried on the wind like music. The Doonagan family had not just returned—they had rooted, built, and called others home with them.

That evening, the townsfolk gathered for a celebration, the kind born not of planning, but of instinct. Long tables were set up in the meadow beyond the croft, piled with bread, roasted meats, and jams glinting like amethysts in the setting sun. Fiddles sang, boots stomped, children ran wild between the legs of dancers.

Maree stood at the edge of it all, watching her siblings and neighbours twirl, laugh, and toast beneath a banner of dusk. The air smelled of woodsmoke, heather, and rain-washed stone. Yet her heart beat with a rhythm separate from the music.

Elspeth stood beside her, silent but alert, like a tree that remembers storms long past. "There's a shift comin', lass," she murmured. "Tonight, the veil thins."

Maree didn't respond. She could feel it too.

As twilight deepened, Fiona and Elspeth slipped away to a quiet patch of moorland, where the winds spoke without interruption. They sat cross-legged beneath a lone Rowan tree, listening not with their ears but with something deeper. Fiona's hand found Elspeth's. No words passed between them—only understanding.

A low wind stirred around them, curling through the Rowan leaves like a whispered breath. Elspeth's lips moved silently, mouthing words in a forgotten tongue. Fiona closed her eyes, and a faint hum rose from her chest—an ancient note, pure and clear, that resonated with the stones nearby. Something stirred in the soil beneath them.

Angus, standing among the revellers, caught sight of Fiona's retreat and smiled quietly to himself. Something in her presence grounded him in a way he'd never thought possible.

As the moon crested the hills and the celebration burned on, Maree slipped away from the croft and into her bed, her limbs heavy but her mind alive with tension she couldn't name.

* * *

In the realm of sleep, the world softened—and then sharpened.

Maree stood alone on a heather-covered hilltop. The air shimmered with silver light, and every blade of grass seemed to breathe. Around her, the land undulated like a slow-moving tide, alive and ancient. Mist curled like fingers through the stones.

And then he came.

Out of the haze stepped a figure cloaked in earth and sky. The Ancient Celt. His garments bore the purples of heather and the dark greens of moss. His tunic was laced with symbols that shifted when she tried to read them. On his brow sat a circlet of vine and bone, and his eyes—his eyes held the whole of time.

Maree tried to speak, but no sound passed her lips.

He raised a hand.

"Ye walk in the wakin' world wi' yer hands in the soil," he said, voice low and vast, "but yer soul belongs tae the stones."

She felt herself drawn toward him, the wind lifting her hair as though in silent welcome.

"There's been a breakin'," he continued. "Long ago, the balance was shattered. Blood spilt where none should've been. The land remembers. It weeps beneath yer feet."

The ground trembled. Stones began to glow with an inner fire, revealing a ring of symbols encircling them both. The same ones she'd seen in her waking life.

"Ye're of the auld line," he said. "The croft is nae accident. The moors chose ye. An' now, they waken."

The Celt turned and beckoned her toward a standing stone, taller than the rest. As they approached, the surface began to shimmer, revealing an etched map—spirals, constellations, rivers, moons.

Maree's fingers hovered over the stone, but the Celt touched her wrist.

"No' yet. The path will unfold in trials. Each step will test yer kin, an' bind yer blood tae the land once more."

She looked up into his face. "Why me?" she whispered at last.

The Celt smiled—soft, sad, proud. "Because the hearth burns brightest when it's lit by the hand that never sought glory."

He stepped back, his figure dissolving into mist and light. The standing stones pulsed once, then stilled.

Maree gasped and sat upright in bed.

Her chest heaved. The fire in the hearth had burned down to embers, but light danced in the corners of the room. She looked to her hand.

A smudge of dirt. And clutched in her palm, a small carved stone. One she hadn't fallen asleep with.

Outside, the moors rustled with quiet reverence. The land had spoken. And Maree had heard it.

In the morning, she kept the stone close, tucked beneath her shawl as she moved through the day. She didn't speak of the dream—not yet—but her eyes searched the faces of her kin for signs that they, too, had been stirred.

Later, by the well, Caitriona paused mid-step, her gaze locked on a spiral-shaped lichen growing across the stone. "It's in my books," she muttered. "But it's movin'..."

Isla, tuning her fiddle, found her fingers playing a tune she didn't remember learning. "It's like I kent it before I was born," she whispered, half-afraid to meet Elspeth's eyes.

Fergus walked the upper ridge and stopped cold when he saw a hawk circling above the same knoll from his childhood. It dipped once, twice, then vanished into mist.

Ewan, checking the fence line, found stones laid out in a pattern he didn't recall placing. A perfect spiral. "They're callin' us," he said aloud, though no one was there to hear.

And Elspeth, in the hush of her garden, whispered to the breeze, "Aye, it's beginnin'. The dream's passed into wakin' now."

SONGS OF STONES, WHISPERS OF MOORS

The dawn mist curled along the moorland path as the Doonagan family made their way toward the standing stones, guided by the dream Maree could not shake. The air crackled—not with cold, but with presence. The very earth beneath their feet felt alive, watchful.

No one spoke. Even Isla's fingers, usually twitching for a tune, rested still.

The standing stones rose from the land like ancient sentinels. As the family approached, a soft wind stirred the heather—and from it, the figure of the Ancient Celt appeared.

He did not walk. He emerged.

Tall and robed in the colours of dusk and peat, he shimmered like moonlight on dark water. His eyes—deep and firelit—held the weight of forgotten centuries.

Maree stepped forward, her voice low with reverence. "Ye came tae me in a dream. What is it these stones want from us? What wrong are we called tae mend?"

The Celt's voice rose like wind through a hollow glen.

"Ye walk upon wounded land. No' from fire or blade—but from forgettin'. Once, your folk walked in harmony with the spirits. But the song was broken. The moors ache still."

Isla stepped forward, clutching her fiddle. "Can the music bring the harmony back? The auld song?"

The Celt's head tilted. "Play no' tae remember. Play tae waken. The moors ken the tune—they're waitin' for the first note."

Fergus, brows drawn, said, "What dangers lie ahead? Will we face storms like before?"

The Celt's smile held no comfort. "Some storms come from sky an' sea. Others rise from within. Ye'll face both."

Caitriona looked up. "The symbols—on the stones, in the dream. How do we read them?"

"They're no words. They're echoes," he said. "Let yer breath slow. Let yer hands learn. The land teaches what tongues forget."

More questions came—Ewan's about the land's limits. Dougal's about his place in it. Fiona's about balance. Angus stayed silent, watching, eyes sharp.

The Celt's answers came in riddles and feeling, not fact.

Then the mist thickened, and between the stones, a shimmer spread like a curtain being drawn back. Before them bloomed a vision—not a flat memory, but a living dream, humming with sorrow.

They saw the old ways. A thriving community—Celts walking the hills barefoot, hands deep in the earth, voices lifted in chant and story. Children danced by sacred springs. Elder guides carved runes into bark. The land breathed with them.

Then came the invaders.

Clad in metal and greed, they came. They tore down trees that bled white sap. Dug into hills with no heed. Dried up the streams. The Celts fought—but the magic, once shared, shrank back.

The guardians—the luminous spirits—faded. The heather lost its colour. The air turned still.

Fiona gasped, a hand to her chest.

Elspeth's eyes shimmered. "Aye," she whispered. "I've heard these cries—in the wind, in the stillness after the storm."

One figure in the vision caught Maree's eye—a woman robed in violet, hand pressed to the very stone she now stood before. Her face lined, yet fierce. She wept as the grove behind her fell.

Maree dropped to her knees. Dougal reached to steady her, but she waved him off.

"Nae," she whispered. "Let me feel it."

The vision faded slowly. The silence that followed was deeper than quiet—it was sacred.

The Celt's voice returned, low and sure. "The land remembers. But it doesnae hate. It grieves. An' it calls for healin'."

He turned to Maree. "Ye are of her line. The woman in violet. Her blood runs in yers. The moors have chosen. Will ye answer?"

Maree looked up, eyes shining. "Aye. We all will."

One by one, the family stepped forward. Fergus whispered an oath. Isla let her fiddle sing a low note. Caitriona rested a leather-bound book at the stone's base. Angus pressed his brow to the stone.

Maree, hand steady, whispered, "We remember. We'll mend what's been broken."

The Celt began to fade, the wind lifting him like ash on the breeze. His voice lingered:

"Redemption is no' found. It's forged."

The family stayed a long while in silence. When they finally turned away, the stones behind them pulsed once with light.

The moors had begun to sing again.

As they descended the hill, the mist parted just enough to reveal a ring of rowan trees at the base of the moor. The trees hadn't bloomed in years, yet now their branches held small, flame-coloured berries.

"It's a sign," Fiona whispered. "The land's respondin' already."

Dougal glanced over his shoulder, back at the stones. "Then we'd best keep movin'. There's more tae uncover."

They continued in quiet procession, each carrying something from the moment—Fergus with a stone, Isla with a tune, Caitriona scribbling runes into her journal. And Maree, still clutching the vision, felt a fire kindle in her chest.

The moors had remembered them. Now, they would remember the moors.

REDEMPTION BEGINS

The weight of responsibility settled heavily upon the family as they stood among the ancient stones.

For a long moment, nobody spoke.

The moors stretched around them beneath a vast Highland sky, beautiful and timeless. Yet now they could see what had always been hidden beneath the surface—the scars left by neglect, greed, and generations who had forgotten how to listen to the land.

Maree rested her hand against one of the standing stones.

The etched symbols seemed almost alive beneath her fingertips.

"We cannae change the past," she said quietly.

"Nay," Ewan agreed.

"But we can change what comes next."

The others nodded.

For the first time since discovering the ancient etchings, the path ahead felt clear.

Not easy.

But clear.

Their work began the following morning.

The family split into groups, each following clues revealed by the standing stones and the wisdom preserved within the ancient writings.

Some sites were small.

Others required days of labour.

All bore evidence of wounds inflicted upon the land.

Angus stood beside a stream that had long ago been diverted from its natural course.

The water trickled weakly through a narrow channel, robbed of its former strength.

He crouched near the bank, studying the damage.

"It reminds me of the Amazon."

Dougal glanced up from the tools he was carrying.

"The Amazon?"

Angus nodded.

"I've seen rivers there choked by greed. Forests stripped bare. Villages displaced."

He looked across the Highland landscape.

"I never imagined I'd see the same thing here."

The words lingered.

Because everyone understood.

The problem wasn't Scotland.

The problem was forgetting.

Forgetting that land was something to care for rather than conquer.

Together, they set to work.

Stone by stone.

Hour by hour.

The stream gradually found its voice again.

Elsewhere, Fergus and Ewan tackled one of the sacred groves.

At first, the brothers worked in silence.

Which was usually a dangerous sign.

Eventually Fergus straightened and wiped sweat from his brow.

"Ye've always thought ye were right."

Ewan rolled his eyes.

"Because I usually am."

Fergus laughed.

"There it is."

The familiar exchange eased something between them.

As children they had raced through these woods.

As men they had drifted onto different paths.

Now, side by side, they found themselves working toward the same purpose once more.

"Da would've liked this."

The words slipped out before Fergus realised he had spoken them aloud.

Ewan paused.

For a moment neither brother moved.

"Aye," Ewan said softly.

"He would've."

The silence that followed felt less painful than before.

Almost comforting.

Not far away, Isla and Caitriona worked among the heather-covered hills.

The sisters carried baskets filled with young plants, carefully restoring areas damaged by years of neglect.

"Do ye remember Mam's garden?" Isla asked suddenly.

Caitriona smiled.

"The one she swore she could manage herself?"

"Aye."

"The one Da secretly helped with every evening?"

Both sisters laughed.

The memory warmed them.

Arabella's flowers had never grown in perfect rows.

They had flourished in cheerful disorder.

Rather like the family itself.

As they planted fresh heather across the hillside, the conversation flowed easily between them.

Stories.

Memories.

Laughter.

The land was not the only thing healing.

Elspeth moved among them all.

Offering advice.

Sharing old stories.

Occasionally directing people away from mistakes before they made them.

No one questioned how she always seemed to know where she was needed.

They had long since accepted that Elspeth possessed her own understanding of the Highlands.

At one particular clearing she stopped.

The wind stirred gently around her.

"This place remembers sorrow."

Maree looked around.

The clearing appeared ordinary.

Yet she trusted Elspeth's instincts.

"What happened here?"

The old woman sighed.

"Long ago, people stopped listening."

Her gaze travelled across the moors.

"That's usually where trouble begins."

Together they planted fresh heather throughout the clearing.

A simple act.

Yet somehow it felt important.

Like restoring a forgotten promise.

Days passed.

The work continued.

The family grew tired.

Aching muscles became commonplace.

Blisters appeared.

Arguments surfaced.

Then disappeared again.

Yet with each passing day the moors responded.

Not dramatically.

Not magically.

Gradually.

A little more birdsong.

A little more colour.

A little more life.

The changes were subtle enough that a stranger might never notice.

But the family noticed.

Because they had become part of the healing.

One afternoon, children from the nearby village arrived carrying small tools and eager smiles.

Word of the restoration had spread throughout the glen.

Soon the youngsters were helping plant heather and clear pathways.

Elspeth gathered them around during a break.

"Want tae hear a story?"

The answer came immediately.

"Aye!"

Before long she was spinning tales of Highland heroes, mischievous spirits, brave crofters, and ancient mysteries.

The children listened with wide eyes.

Maree watched from nearby.

A smile touched her lips.

Perhaps this was how it began.

Not merely by restoring the land.

But by passing its stories forward.

That evening the family gathered around a great bonfire atop the central hill.

The flames danced against the darkness.

Mugs of broth passed from hand to hand.

The stars emerged overhead.

One by one.

For a while they simply sat together.

Content.

Exhausted.

Happy.

The fire crackled.

Laughter drifted across the hillside.

Fiona gazed out over the moors.

"They feel different."

"They are different," Dougal replied.

"Nay."

She smiled.

"I mean us."

Nobody argued.

Because she was right.

The journey had changed them all.

Maree looked around the circle.

Her family.

Her friends.

The people she loved.

For so long she had believed the standing stones had led her toward ancient mysteries.

Perhaps they had.

But now she suspected Dee they had led her toward something even more important.

Each other.

The wind moved gently through the heather.

The moors whispered their eternal song.

And for the first time in many years, Maree felt peace settle within her heart.

Not the peace that comes from endings.

But the peace that comes from knowing a new beginning has finally arrived.

LEGACY OF THE HIGHLANDS

In the wake of their restoration efforts, the Doonagan family returned to their crofts, their bodies weary but their spirits uplifted. The moors, once marred by the wounds of time, now stood as a testament to the family's commitment to the Highland way of life. Although physically drained, the sense of fulfilment that washed over them became a balm for the tiredness that lingered.

As the family rested, Elspeth, with a spirit as ageless as the moors themselves, continued her nocturnal dances beneath the moonlight. Her steps, light as heather on the breeze, echoed the joy that had infused the Highland air. With every twirl, she communed with the ancient whispers that wove through the landscape, a celebration of the harmony restored to the moors.

* * *

Days passed before the family emerged from their well-deserved respite. Their faces, etched with the lines of effort, now held a serene glow, a reflection of the profound connection forged with the land. Maree, her eyes gazing over the newly revitalised moors, spoke with a depth that echoed the sentiments of the clan.

"Our journey has been one of redemption, and in that redemption, we have found our purpose. Our lives are intertwined with the heartbeat of the Highlands, and it's our duty to keep that rhythm alive. Love, nurture, and understanding shall be our offerings to all who seek solace within these sacred moors."

In the wake of their vow, the Doonagan family embraced a life dedicated to maintaining the balance between nature and humanity. Their crofts became beacons of Highland harmony, welcoming both villagers and wanderers with open arms. The family's commitment to the land, now etched into the very fabric of their existence, formed a legacy that would endure through generations—a tapestry woven with threads of love, resilience, and the enduring spirit of the moors.

Maree, standing alongside Elspeth, gazed out over the rejuvenated moors. The winds carried whispers of gratitude, and the heather, vibrant against the Highland backdrop, seemed to nod in agreement. Elspeth, her eyes reflecting the dance of the flames in her hearth, spoke with a wisdom as ancient as the stones beneath their feet.

"Ye see lass, if the storms hadn't come, the guide stones and ancient structures never would have been uncovered. It took two of the biggest storms known to this area to reveal its secrets. And in revealing these wounds, coupled with the return of yer siblings, all the ingredients were finally together to create this wonder ye have done!"

Elspeth's joy radiated through her words.

Maree, exhaustion and satisfaction etched into every line of her face, nodded once—slow and sure. "Aye, Elspeth. It was a journey of storms and revelations, but in the end, we found the path to redemption."

Elspeth's laughter, a melody in sync with the moorland winds, echoed through the air. "Redemption indeed, and a gift to the moors that will be felt for generations to come. Ye have become stewards of the Highland spirit, and the ancient guides look upon ye with favour."

* * *

The Doonagan family and their companions gathered once again at the ancient Standing Stones, the air charged with anticipation. Elspeth, the keeper of the moors' secrets, stood before the stones, her eyes reflecting the wisdom of the Highlands. The family, having completed their task of restoring the sacred balance, approached her with a shared curiosity.

"Elspeth," Ewan spoke, his voice a blend of reverence and excitement, "will the Altar of the Highland Veil welcome us once more? We wish to gaze upon the wonders beyond and pay respects to our ancestors."

Elspeth nodded, her gaze meeting each member of the family. "Aye, the Altar recognises the kin who have tended to the moors' wounds. The stones will guide ye once more."

As if in response to Elspeth's words, the ancient Standing Stones began to resonate with a subtle vibration. The air around them shimmered, and a soft glow emanated from the stones. Slowly, the surface of one of the stones shifted, revealing an intricate pattern that seemed to guide the way.

The family exchanged eager glances as the stones formed a pathway leading to a concealed stairway beneath them. The steps, bathed in a warm, ethereal light, invited them to descend into the mysteries of the Altar of the Highland Veil.

With Elspeth leading the way, the family descended the stairway, the air around them growing more charged with magic with each step. As they passed through the veil, the landscape transformed into a realm of unparalleled beauty.

Fields of heather stretched in vibrant hues, and the hills undulated in colours that surpassed the earthly spectrum. The sky above was an ever-changing canvas, displaying the dance of celestial lights in breathtaking patterns. A gentle breeze carried the fragrance of heather, and the air seemed to resonate with an unseen melody.

Music, both haunting and joyous, surrounded them. The harmonies of unseen instruments played in perfect cadence with the heartbeat of the moors. The family found themselves in a symphony of nature, where every note told stories of ancient times, resilience, and the enduring spirit of the Highlands.

As they journeyed through this enchanting realm, they encountered mystical beings—a stag with antlers that sparkled like starlight, butterflies with wings that reflected the colours of the heather, and luminous creatures that danced among the blooms. The air was filled with the gentle laughter of unseen spirits, and the wonders of the Altar unfolded with each step.

In the heart of the Altar, they discovered a serene space where time itself seemed to pause. The Altar pulsated with energy, adorned with carvings that depicted the family's journey of restoration. And there, in the midst of the magical landscape, appeared the loving forms of Duncan and Arabella, the beloved parents of the Doonagan siblings.

For a breathless moment, time itself seemed to pause, the veil between worlds held open by love alone.

Tears welled in the eyes of the family as they embraced their parents. Laughter and joy echoed through the Altar as Duncan and Arabella expressed their pride and love for their adult children. The reunion transcended the boundaries between the mortal and mystical realms, and for a fleeting moment, the family shared the warmth of hugs and the familiarity of laughter.

As he spoke, Duncan approached each of his bairns with a warmth that transcended the boundary between the mystical and mortal realms. He hugged them separately, looking each one in the face, cupping their heads, and kissing them on the forehead. The embrace carried the essence of a father's love, an affirmation that echoed through the Altar's sacred space. Each sibling, touched by the tangible connection with their spectral father, felt a profound sense of reassurance and love in that moment.

In a tender display of maternal love, Arabella gathered her five children into her arms. One by one, she stroked their hair, loving on them for a while, and then leaned back, cradling the cherished moment in the embrace of the Altar's mystical ambience. "I'm so proud of you, my beloved bairns. Against all odds, an' counting tae cost and sacrifice, ye've done what no others would dare tae. I'm forever grateful fir ye all."

Dougal lingered at the edge of the Altar longer than the others, his eyes glistening as he took in the sight of the parents his beloved Maree had often described, though he had never met them in life. Duncan crossed the space slowly and rested a hand on Dougal's shoulder, his voice low and full of warmth. "Ye've stood by our daughter wi' honour, son. We've watched over ye, even if ye never knew." Dougal swallowed hard, nodding, his throat tight. In that moment, the embrace he returned wasn't for himself—but for Maree, for the family he had joined, and for the bond he now felt, strong and true.

Angus and Fiona, hands entwined, knelt before Duncan and Arabella, offering words of thanks not just for their blessing, but for the strength their legacy had breathed into the clan. Arabella bent low and kissed both their foreheads, her touch light, but her presence unmistakably real. "Ye belong tae this family," she whispered. "By blood, by choice, by love."

Caitriona stepped forward next, her ancient tomes tucked beneath one arm, her free hand reaching for her mother's. "Will the stories remember us?" she asked, voice quiet. Arabella smiled and placed her hand over Caitriona's heart. "They already do."

Fergus, ever the wanderer, looked to Duncan with a boyish grin. "Still got the sea in me, Da. But it's here I come home." Duncan clapped a hand to his shoulder, eyes crinkling. "An' may the sea always bring ye back, lad."

Ewan, the eldest, stood back a moment, letting the others step forward first. Then he approached, arms folded, pride and pain etched deep into his face. Duncan pulled him into a firm embrace and held him tightly. "Ye led them home, son. That's what a true elder does." And for once, Ewan let himself be held, a tear finally tracing down his cheek.

Elspeth stood slightly apart, tears in her eyes as she watched the family gather, love binding every word and gesture. Isobel approached her last and took her hands in her own. "Ye were their shield and their strength, Elspeth. The moors will speak your name for generations."

As the family gathered one last time in the sacred glade, the wind picked up, lifting hair and cloak alike. It swirled around them in a final embrace, carrying the songs of the stones, the love of their ancestors, and the promise of all that was still to come.

The family prepared to ascend the stairway and return to the mortal realm, Duncan and Arabella bid their children farewell with loving smiles. The Altar responded to their departure, and the ethereal light guided the family back through the veil.

Emerging from the concealed stairway, the family found themselves once again at the ancient Standing Stones. The stones seemed to hum with a contented energy, and the air was charged with the magic of the Altar's blessings. The family, touched by the wonders they had witnessed and the reunion with their parents, stood united in the heart of the Highlands, their spirits forever intertwined with the mysteries of the moors.

Maree and Dougal walked back to their croft, they warmly invited everyone to gather, sup, and share tales of their incredible adventure beneath the stones. The croft, bathed in the glow of the setting sun, stood as a testament to the resilience, unity, and newly endowed magic of the Doonagan family. The hearth fires burned with a warmth that transcended the physical, carrying the echoes of Highland harmony.

The legacy of the moors—rekindled, reawakened, and rooted in love—now awaited the unfolding tales the winds would carry across the heathered hills, whispering them into legend.

EPILOGUE

The fire had burned low in the hearth, its embers glowing softly as the croft settled into quiet slumber. Outside, the Highland mist drifted lazily across the moors, whispering through the heather as though carrying the last echoes of the family's great journey. Inside, nestled beneath a thick woollen blanket, Fiona stirred restlessly. Sleep had claimed her, but her mind was far from the warmth of her home.

She dreamed.

In the dream, she sat in the back of a horse-drawn cart, the wooden wheels creaking over a well-worn road. The air smelled different—not of the Highlands, but of distant lands, damp earth, and something older, something forgotten. She glanced around and saw Maree beside her, bundled against the cold, her eyes fixed on the horizon with quiet determination. Angus held the reins, guiding the horses through the shifting mist, while Dougal sat beside him, silent, his posture tense as though he were bracing for something unseen.

The cart was heavy with gear—trunks filled with belongings, blankets, tools, and provisions. This was no simple journey. They were moving, uprooting. But to where?

As the mist parted, Fiona saw it.

A great estate loomed ahead, its silhouette stark against the muted sky. The house—if it could still be called that—was vast, its stone walls crumbling, ivy climbing like skeletal fingers over the once-grand facade. The windows were dark, empty, like eyes that had long since stopped seeing. Towers jutted upward, their peaks lost in the mist, while broken shutters dangled from rusted hinges. A place abandoned, yet waiting. A place forgotten, yet calling.

Her heart pounded. She looked to Dougal, who had stopped the cart at the edge of the overgrown drive. He had climbed down and was now walking toward the estate, his pace slow, hesitant. His fingers brushed against the cold stone of a weathered archway as though testing its reality. There was something in his stance, something in the way his head tilted as he studied the ruins, that sent a shiver through Fiona.

He knew this place.

Or worse—it knew him.

The wind howled through the open halls, sending a scattering of dead leaves spiralling through the air. The heavy wooden doors groaned as if they longed to open but were held shut by the weight of years. A whisper curled through the mist, just barely audible.

Come home.

Fiona gasped, jolting upright in bed, her breath ragged. The croft was still, the only sound the faint crackling of the dying fire. She pressed a trembling hand to her chest, trying to shake the lingering dread of the dream. But the image of the ruined estate, of Dougal standing before it as though drawn by an unseen force, would not leave her.

She turned her head toward the hearth, eyes catching the dull gleam of her boots near the door. For a moment, her hand drifted to the pendant at her neck, fingers tightening around it as though bracing herself.

She knew with absolute certainty—this was not just a dream.

It was a warning.

Not a call to action, not yet. But a whisper that the story was not over.

The moors had been healed, yes—but they were not the only place bearing wounds. And though peace had settled like a soft shawl across their croft, Fiona knew it would not remain forever.

The dream had planted something. A question. A memory. Perhaps even a seed.

In the quiet morning that followed, Fiona rose early and slipped outside. The heather was slick with dew, and the mist curled around her boots like a familiar friend. The wind no longer whispered but hummed, low and constant, like the overture of a tale yet untold.

She walked to the standing stones, drawn by an instinct she couldn't explain. The earth beneath her feet felt different, awake. The stones stood silent, but the space between them shimmered faintly, like breath caught between worlds. She reached out, her palm brushing the ancient surface—and felt warmth.

Behind her, soft footsteps approached. Maree stood beside her, followed closely by Dougal and Angus, their expressions thoughtful. Not solemn, but curious. They too had felt something—a stirring, a murmur beneath the roots of the earth.

"It felt like a thread was tugged," Maree said softly. "No' a command. Just... a reminder. Dat there's more still hidden."

Angus ran a hand through his hair. "We've awakened somethin', that's for sure. But maybe it's not askin' us to run off straight away. Maybe it's just whisperin' so we dinnae forget."

Fiona nodded, her fingers still resting on the stone. "It's not a summons. No' yet. It's a promise. Dat when dae time comes, we'll know."

They stood there a moment longer, letting the mist wrap around them like an embrace.

Then, together, they turned back toward the croft. There would be time. When the call came again, they would be ready. But for now, the moors were quiet—and so were they.

ALSO BY DEE WHITMAN

Guardians of Clachanoch: *Heirs of the Highland, Book Two*

Legacy of the Lost Clans: *Heirs of the Highland, Book Three*

Outback Shadows

The Frontier Dance

The Frontier Christmas - *Coming Soon!*

The Frontier Reckoning - *Coming Soon!*

Call of the Ancients

Lord Ashton's Enchantment - *Coming Soon!*